HIROSHIMA

Chronicles
of a
Survivor

by
Katharine Johnson

with
John F. Rasche

BRANDEN BOOKS
Branden Publishing Company, Inc.

Library of Congress Cataloging-in-Publication Data

Johnson, Katharine, 1894-1959.
    Hiroshima : chronicles of a survivor / by Katharine
Johnson with John F. Rasche.
        p. cm.
    Includes bibliographical references and index.
    ISBN 0-8283-2001-2
        1.Hiroshima-shi(Japan)--History--Bombardment,
1945--Fiction.
        2. World War, 1939-1945--Japan--Hiroshima-shi--
Fiction.
        3. Schools--Japan--Hiroshima-shi--Fiction.
    I. Rasche, John F.
    II. Title.
PS3560.0379545H57 1994
813'.54--dc20   94-20245
                                                        CIP

BRANDEN BOOKS
Branden Publishing Company, Inc.
17 Station Street
Box 843 Brookline Village
Boston, MA 02147

DEDICATION

This book is dedicated to the memory of its author, Miss Katharine Johnson, and to the students, faculty and friends of Hiroshima Jogakuin who died or suffered as a result of the atomic bombing in Hiroshima.

CONTENTS

ACKNOWLEDGEMENTS

First, I would like to thank my wife, Judy, for her support and understanding of the time involved in publishing this book.

To my aunt, Mrs. G. Roland (Mildred Johnson) Sims, who preserved this manuscript and a photo album for many years. She also helped me locate sources for research and shared stories about her sister, Katharine Johnson.

To Ms. G. Loraine Harriott, Assistant Records Manager, Central Records Office of the General Board of Global Ministries, The United Methodist Church, who located a tremendous amount of information related to Nannie B. Gaines, Katharine Johnson, and the school.

To Mrs. Ruth Kurtz, Director of Promotion Utilization, General Board of Missions of the United Methodist Church, for her help in obtaining permission to use information from several church sources.

To Mrs. Helen Wiegel, Director, Peace Resource Center, Wilmington College (Ohio), for reading the manuscript and for writing the Foreword for this book.

To Ms. Pat Walt from Peace Resource Center, for her help in locating Hiroshima and Hiroshima Jogakuin literature.

To Miss Mary Jo Thompson who shared information about Miss Johnson, including a letter she wrote to friends at Wesleyan College in 1951.

To Mrs. Elizabeth S. Akers who shared her memories about Miss Johnson.

Many of the pictures used in this book were located in a photo album which was in Katharine Johnson's possession at the time of her death. It was given to the J.B. Cain Archives at Millsaps College, Jackson, Mississippi. Ms. Debra McIntosh, College Archivist, was very helpful with the photo album and providing information about the Lambuth family. Also, Mrs. Herman McKinzie helped me locate research sources.

Other pictures are from books published by Hiroshima Jogakuin, *Hiroshima Jogakuin, Eighty Years of History in Pictures, Hiroshima Jogakuin, 1886-1986*, and *Hiroshima Jogakuin, 1987.* I am indebted to Professor Masuyuki Imaishi, Chairman of the Board (retired March 1994), Hiroshima Jogakuin College for permission to use these pictures and for other information and pictures he sent me. Mrs. Yuko Kato shared picture number 12 of the Matsumoto family.

To Mrs. Shirley Brooks who reviewed the manuscript and gave advice on grammar and style.

To Mr. Adolpho Caso, Editor, Branden Publishing Company, Inc. for his patience with me and his considerable help as this manuscript was compiled.

Many others have been very helpful in my research, including Dr. R.K. Ackerman, president of Wesleyan College; Ms. Tena Roberts, librarian at Wesleyan College; Ms. Linda Nelson, Coordinator of Alumni Programs Central Methodist College; Mr. Donald Underwood, Director of Alumni Programs, Teachers College, Columbia University; Dr. Robert Drew Simpson and Mr. Dale Patterson, General Commission on Archives and History, The United Methodist Church; Ms. Maxine Hunsinger Sullivan, University Registrar, The University of Chicago; Ms. Martha S. Pilcher, administrator, The Scarritt Foundation; Ms. Patricia J. Patterson, JNAC Coordinator, Japan-North American Commission on Cooperative Mission, and several friends who have advised me.

John F. Rasche,
compiler of supplemental information
(nephew of Katharine Johnson)

FOREWORD

Hiroshima: Chronicles of a Survivor fills a unique niche in the field of A-bomb literature. I have read many books about the atomic bombings of Hiroshima and Nagasaki, but this is the first I have found which gives such an intimate picture of the city and its people **before** the destruction of August 6, 1945.

Although technically a work of fiction, the book focuses on the staff and students of Hiroshima Girls' School, a very real institution where Katharine Johnson was a teacher until the approach of wartime forced her and other missionaries to return to the U.S. This obvious tie to reality suffuses the book, giving special meaning to all its characters.

Moving at a leisurely pace, with exquisite attention to the minutiae of daily life, the author brings to life the various people in the story. In beautifully painted word pictures we see and feel what the city was like on those hot August days. Flashbacks bring in information about earlier years of the school, but inexorably we are moved closer and closer to 8:15 a.m. on August 6.

Unlike most other A-bomb books, only brief accounts are given of how the explosion affected the various characters in the book. In the Epilogue and other appendices, the focus shifts from how the school and the persons connected with it coped during wartime, to what happened after the war and what the status of the schools is today.

I have visited Hiroshima Jogakuin (Women's) College in the hills of Ushita, as well as the Junior High and Senior High campus in downtown Hiroshima. I have walked the streets and parks of the new Hiroshima. I am grateful for the "inside look"

10--Katharine Johnson

at the schools given by this book, and for the new mental picture I now have of Hiroshima prior to its destruction on August 6, 1945.

Helen D. Wiegel,
Director Hiroshima/Nagasaki Memorial Collection
Wilmington College, Ohio

INTRODUCTION

John F. Rasche

The memories of my aunt, Katharine Johnson, author of this book, are probably typical of the memories of many of you for a special aunt. They do not include extensive knowledge about her life, her experiences as a teacher in Japan and in the United States, the effect of the atomic bomb on the people and the school in Hiroshima, etc. These things came later, the result of research long after her death.

I knew her as "Kaki," the name affectionately used by all in her extended family. My sister, Katharine, was named for her. We lived in Missouri, she in Hiroshima, Georgia and New York. Our contacts were not frequent, however I eagerly anticipated her visits. I was four years old in 1940 when she returned to the United States 18 years after first going to Hiroshima. She lived in the United States most of the rest of her life. I graduated from college and was married in 1958, less than a year before her death, so my relationship was that of a young person.

Some of my memories of Kaki follow. She was a friendly and cheerful friend who often brought interesting presents from far away places. I still have an abacus which was one of those gifts. She identified with children and youth - I remember that she once told me she had heard the song, "The Doggie in the Window" (Patti Page pop hit in 1953) and wondered if I had heard it. I remember meeting her on August 11, 1952 at the age of 16 at a San Francisco dock as she walked down the gang plank of a ship, and eating together at a Fisherman's Wharf restaurant. She was returning from a 15 month period as vice president of Hiroshima Jogakuin. Our family was on a six week trip through the western United States. The trip was planned to coincide with her arrival. I was impressed on several occasions by all the tags tied to her luggage, the results of her extensive travel.

About fifteen years ago, my cousin, Gibson Sims, brought Kaki's manuscript for this book to me. His mother, Mildred Johnson Sims, had kept the manuscript since Kaki's death. I knew about the manuscript - that it was written soon after the atomic bomb was dropped on Hiroshima, that Kaki had plans for publication with a publisher, and that the plans were dropped because John Hersey's book, *Hiroshima*, came out before her manuscript was complete.

This was the first time that I had seen the manuscript, and reading it was fascinating to me. In the book, she writes about the school and people whom she knew well in Hiroshima.

Those of us who read it believe it tells an important story which should be shared with others. We are happy that Branden Publishing Company, Inc. agreed to publish it at this time, nearly 50 years since the atomic bomb was dropped on Hiroshima.

Numerous books have been written about this historic event. Many of these are powerfully written, thought provoking and touching as they describe the impact of the atomic bomb on the people living in Hiroshima. This book, however, seems unique in its emphasis on the people and their lives before the bomb fell. It also shares the impact of the school, Hiroshima Jogakuin, on many of the characters in the book. Readers come away with a deep understanding of the people so greatly affected by the atomic bomb.

I have gathered facts, stories and pictures, to provide the reader with supplemental information about the school and people connected to it. Most of this material is located in the epilogue and the reader may want to delay reading it until finishing the story.

From what I have been able to check, major events in Miss Johnson's story are factual. References to Gaines Sensei and Miss Rachel refer to the historical persons, Miss Nannie B. Gaines and her sister, Miss Rachel G. Gaines. Miss Nannie B. Gaines helped the school grow soon after its founding in 1886 until her death on February 26, 1932. Miss Johnson used fictional names for other characters and disguised events to protect the privacy of her friends.

THE AUTHOR
THROUGH WORLD WAR II

Katharine Johnson was born August 27, 1894, in Poplar Bluff, Missouri, the daughter of Rev. Alfred Crosby Johnson and Mary Katharine Yancey Johnson. Her father was a Methodist minister in Missouri. Both her grandfathers were attorneys and each represented the 24th Senatorial District of Missouri for a four year term. Senator Charles D. Yancey lived in Piedmont and was elected in 1882 and Senator J. Perry Johnson lived in Fredericktown when elected in 1886. Senator Johnson later moved his law offices and family to Poplar Bluff, Missouri.

When Katharine was four years old, her mother died at their home in Centralia, Missouri, on May 14, 1899, apparently as a result of a stillbirth. Katharine then lived with her father's parents in Poplar Bluff for two years until her father married Mattie Willeta Collett on June 11, 1901, in Fulton, Missouri.

The family grew, with the addition of three sisters, Addie, Margaret and Mildred. Her father served Missouri churches in Hannibal, Maryville, Richmond, and then Fulton where Katharine graduated from Fulton High School in 1912. Her family moved to Fayette in 1912 for four years and Katharine obtained her AA Degree from Howard Payne College (for women) in 1914, and an AB degree in language, English and history from Central College in 1916.

The family returned to Fulton in 1916 and Katharine taught English and Latin in the high school. She was interested in missionary work from the time she graduated from college and was Superintendent of Young People's Work for the Woman's

Missionary Council of the Missouri Conference. Her family moved to Savannah, Missouri, in 1920 and at about the same time, she decided to be a foreign missionary. She continued to teach the next year in Fulton, but also applied to The Board of Missions of the Methodist Episcopal Church, South for foreign missionary service in October 1920 at the age of 26. Following the 1920-21 year at Fulton High School, she studied at Scarritt Bible and Training School in Kansas City, Missouri, for the school year of 1921-1922 in preparation for work in Japan.

Miss Johnson left for Hiroshima Girls' School in August 1922 and taught English that year. She was the first foreign teacher to serve full time in the College Department, which had opened in 1919. She studied Japanese while in Japan with an elderly Japanese couple and also attended Japanese Language School in Kobe the fall of 1923. In addition to teaching English at the school, she served as Dean of the department during her last five years there. While in Japan, she developed a love for Japanese culture. She was allowed to participate in the tea ceremony when this was an honor for a foreigner. She also appreciated Japanese art and crafts, including prints and paintings, sculpture and porcelain dishes.

Miss Johnson returned to the U.S. three times during her work at Hiroshima Jogakuin. She was in demand for speaking engagements during these times. In addition, she continued her education during the first two of these trips.

She returned in July 1927 for two and a half years. During this time, she studied as a graduate student at Scarritt for the school year 1927-1928, and then at The University of Chicago for the Spring Quarter of 1928 through December 1929 to obtain the degree Master of Arts in Comparative Literature. Her thesis was on "Primitive Japanese Literature in the Writings of Lafcadio Hearn."

Her second furlough was in October 1936 for one year. During this time she took additional education courses at The University of Chicago during the Spring Quarter of 1937.

The third trip home was for three months during the summer of 1940 to visit with her family. Her sisters had married and seven of her nine nieces and nephews were born by this time.

Miss Johnson left Hiroshima Jogakuin in December 1940 with other missionaries because of the approach of World War II, more than 18 years after her arrival in 1922. She was allowed to sell a vacation home in the mountains at Karuizawa and to return her possessions to the U.S. at this time. This was an indication of the respect the Japanese held for her and the school.

She studied at Columbia University for the first nine months of 1941 in preparation for her new position as Dean of Women at Wesleyan College in Macon, Georgia, from 1941 until 1945. The remainder of her career is described in the epilogue.

2. Katharine Johnson with her niece, Katharine Rasche, near the end of World War II.

1. Katharine Johnson before going to Japan.

MAJOR CHARACTERS
IN THE BOOK

Fictional names are used for all but Gaines Sensei and Miss Rachel.

Sensei following a name means teacher. San following a name is used for Mr., Miss or Mrs.

Gaines Sensei - Miss Nannie B. Gaines who helped found the school in 1887 and died in 1932 after nearly 45 years of service to the school.

Miss Rachel - Miss Rachael G. Gaines, sister of Nannie B. Gaines.

Sera Sensei - Long time teacher at the school, daughter of Oka San and a Buddhist priest.

Yamada Sensei - A teacher who came to the school in about 1927 as a Sociology professor after spending four years at Columbia University. He was married with a young son.

Petroff Sensei - A White Russian refugee who started a violin department at the school. He was married with three children.

Mariya Petroff - The wife of Petroff Sensei.

Sandra Petroff - The oldest child of the Petroffs.

Niki Petroff - The oldest son of the Petroffs. He served in the U.S. Army.

Dannie Petroff - The youngest child of the Petroffs.

Hata San - Alumnae secretary at the school. She raised her brother's daughter, Mi-chan, after his wife died in childbirth and was a good friend of Kihara San and Mori San.

Mi-chan - Niece of Hata San. Graduated from the school in 1942. She was married with two children and her husband was a soldier.

Kihara San - A graduate of the school. She was the daughter of wealthy parents who had been merchants in Shanghai. She was a good friend of Hata San and Mori San.

Saburo Kihara - The husband of Kihara San. He was adopted by her parents to continue the family name. He was seeing Hana Chan, a Geisha.

Sa-chan Kihara - The son of the Kiharas. He served in the Japanese Army.

Tamako San - She worked for more than 20 years at the school helping Gaines Sensei and her sister, Miss Rachel. She was living with the Kiharas in the book.

Mori San - She attended school in about 1917. She never married and was a good friend of Hata San and Kihara San. Her father was gatekeeper at the school and a former Samurai for Lord Asano. She came to America twice - to visit Gaines Sensei's home in Kentucky and with Miss Rachel when she returned to the U.S. in early 1945. Some parts of her life in the story represent Miss Kobori.

Yuki San - A servant to Mori San.

Ojii San - When young he fought against China and later against Russia. He was married with two sons. The older son died in 1942 in the China War. The younger son was married to Ayako San and was killed on Okinawa.

Obaa San - The wife of Ojii San.

Ayako San - The daughter-in-law of Ojii San and Obaa San. She lived with them along with her son, Tajiro.

Tajiro - The grandson of Ojii San and Obaa San, son of Ayako San.

Nishida - The manager of a Geisha house.

Hana Chan - A geisha who was seeing Saburo Kihara.

Masako San - A student from the country in the mountains. Her family included her mother and father, grandfather and grandmother, oldest brother and his wife and two children, two younger brothers, two sisters, and two brothers in the army.

Shizuko San - A student and roommate to Masako San. Her home was in Okayama. Her father was an army officer and her mother and little brother lived at home.

Harue - A second year student whose parents lived in a village and farmed. Her brother was in the South Pacific.

CHAPTER 1
MORNING IN HIROSHIMA

The morning of August 6, 1945 began like any other August morning for the city of Hiroshima. Before the gray dawn turned to light, here and there through the city streets there was an early morning stir like the quiet breathing of a living thing asleep. But for the most part, the city still lay quiet in the only cool moments of the day. The sun, of course, was up a fraction later than on the day before, but its progress was the same. Before it reached a height from which it could look down upon the city it lighted up the peaks of mountains that stood in guarding phalanxes, row on row, to the east, the north, the west. Then moving in a rapid sure progression, the sun poured its gold upon the gray roofs of the city and turned the waters of the Inland Sea into a blue summer sky. The city that it looked upon filled all the space between the mountains and the sea. From the north the Ota River flowed like a silver thread drawn through the mountains, now seen, now hidden, until it emerged two rivers just above the city. In their urgency to reach the sea these two divided and again divided until they poured their waters out of seven mouths into the Inland Sea. From above, the rivers looked like the fingers of a great open hand with the city built upon the land that filled the spaces in between the fingers.

The city on this August morning awoke as the sun shone full upon her. She was full of self-pride and complacency. She had seen so many mornings, more than 300 years of them. Sometimes she woke a little tired. But she was proud that people liked to live here on these forks of land between the mountains and the sea. She was proud of her past years, of her great men and the deeds they had done; of princes who had visited her; of her priests, her temples and her shrines. She was most proud of the old feudal castle that stood erect, unchanging in the heart of her. It had withstood the blasts of many wars. She had her pride, too, in the present. Through this day that was beginning, in the shadow of the castle, men would carry on traditions sacred to her as they guided operations in this greatest war of all. She was proud of all the military aid she gave her country, of her shipyards and docks; of her arsenals and factories; her barracks and training grounds. She was proud of her paved streets and her schools, her concrete banks and railway station, and her one department store.

This morning she was conscious of the life that stirred within her. As long as there was growth she knew there would be life. There had always been growth since the first fishermen had settled upon this pleasant delta land. Even now in days like these, there still was growth. War always brought more people to her. This war was long, but it would pass as other wars had passed. When it was over she would be a little shabby and more drab, perhaps, but life would be the more insistent in her. As long as people filled her rivers and her streets with commerce; as long as children were conceived and born within her houses; as long as men and women walked her ways with dreams and aspirations in their souls she would not die. She shook herself through all her streets and houses and faced this day as she had faced a thousand others, with confidence that morning would be followed by a noontide and a night -- and a tomorrow.

In a gray stucco house on the city's Upper Flowing River Street, Mori San turned restlessly upon her pallet. The sea breeze that had made sleep possible a few short hours before was beginning to die down again. It would soon be time to face another day. This seemed more difficult with each new morning. The war moved on, unceasing and relentless. Sometimes she felt that it would crush them all before it ended. But this she must not think about or despair would flood her soul. Great waves of fatigue and loneliness engulfed her. She turned away from the brightness of the window. How foolish of her to be so upset about a day that was so new. She would face the day just as she had faced all other days since this war began. Such tired thoughts came, no doubt, from too little food. Nobody had enough to eat these days, and it was hard for her to eat the little that she had. She must try to eat a little more. She wished her brother would stop writing her to come and stay with him in Yokohama. She was far better off here in Hiroshima. This was her home. Her friends were here. Besides, he had a wife and children to find food for. Here were just the two of them, herself and Yuki San, the servant. Servant? Yuki San was much more than that. For the last three years she had been mother, friend and adviser. She could hear her now downstairs. She must be at her morning cleaning. Yuki did not need to work so hard. For just the two of them there was little work to do. The house was far too large for just the two of them, and she was much too old to sweep and dust the whole house every day. When she went downstairs this morning she would talk to Yuki San about closing up a part of it. When she went downstairs? How much longer could she lie here? At least until it was too hot to lie still any longer. No use to force the day.

Strange how often on these summer mornings she thought first of Gaines Sensei, then of her father. More like a grandfather he had always been. She had been the youngest child, and he was an old man when she first remembered him. The stories he had told her of the days when he was young had made him seem still older. They were always stories of Hiroshima, but she knew nothing about knights and bows and arrows and the falcons they had kept to hunt with. Such stories sounded like the tales of Momotaro who floated down the river to his parents on the inside of a peach seed. From all the things her father told her it seemed her ancestors must have been among the first to settle here. No wonder she felt like such a part of everything. Over and over her father said to her, "Never forget that you are of the samurai!" The samurai. What sorry things the Restoration made of them. Her father had been like all the rest, unlearned in peaceful ways, trained only in the arts of warfare -- bows and swords and falcons. How old and distant it all seemed! She wondered how these modern war-makers would feel if they were suddenly bereft of all their military regalia and told they must live the ordinary life of a civilian. It would be better now because a soldier's training taught him how to do more things. The samurai was never taught to make a living. Because her father had been young and strong when the feudal system fell apart he had received a new jinrikisha as a parting gift from his lord, the Prince Asano. She had never known him as a ricksha man; she had only known him later when his heart was weak and he could run no longer. ---- What was Yuki San about at this hour of the morning? She must be moving all the furniture, and in this heat!

When she first knew her father he was gatekeeper at Gaines Sensei's School. She had been proud of that. Everybody in the city knew about "The School". "Mission" everybody called it. But what "Mission" was no one could ever tell her. Foreign ladies lived there in the big houses behind the red brick wall. Teachers, people said they were. She knew Gaines Sensei's name because she was the one her father always talked about. When she had asked her father what the queer word "Mission" meant he said it was in some way connected with the foreigners' religion. He was not sure about it.

One day her father took her with him when he went to work. All day she sat beside him on the floor of the little gatehouse, just inside the big iron gates, and watched the people come and go. That day she saw her first American. To this day she could not tell whether the excitement she had felt was joy or fear. The foreign lady was a teacher in the school, her father said. What she remembered was someone very tall, dressed all in white, and with yellow hair. All the hair she had seen before was black. That was more than 30 years ago, but lying here this minute in this upstairs room she still could see the yellow hair and feel the cold chills of excitement running up and down her spine.

Often she would take her father's lunch to him. She had loved to walk beside the red brick wall and say, "My school, my father's school." As her father ate the lunch she brought she would sit beside him on the floor and ask him questions. "Why do so many girls come here to school?"

"Because it is a good school and an old one," her father would reply.

"How old?"

"So old there were no other schools for girls in all the city when this one was begun."

"What does Gaines Sensei look like? Does she have yellow hair? Do all Americans have yellow hair?"

All these questions and many more she asked him. Always he was kind and quick to answer. And then one day while she was asking questions she heard a quiet voice call, "Gomenasai! -- Excuse me please!" Her father bowed, head to the floor.

"Oh, Gaines Sensei, please come in," he said. And there she stood, tall and straight, her brown hair piled high upon her head, her soft gray eyes pouring out their kindness on her.

There was a little business talk with her father, and then Gaines Sensei said, "Is this your youngest daughter? She is quite a big girl. Why does she not come here to school?"

"But Sensei," replied her father, "I have no money to send her to school."

"Send her and we shall find some work for her to do." And so she became a part of Gaines Sensei's school.

She liked Gaines Sensei, but she did not like to read the books the teachers gave her. Especially she did not like arithmetic. Three times she left the dormitory and went home to hide. Three times her father found her there. Each time, without a word, he took her by the hand and led her back. She could still hear the stern tones of Gaines Sensei's reprimand. Perhaps it was the kindness in her eyes when there was firmness in her voice that made them all both fear and love her.

If she only had the courage to open her eyes now and see what time it was. The growing heat told her the sun was higher. But the street was quiet still. A few carts had creaked by beyond the red brick wall and the willow tree. The sewage carts had passed before the breeze died down. She had known them by the stench that filled the room. Perhaps when the war was over Hiroshima would have a sewage system. How astonished she had been to learn that such odors were not necessary; that there were other kinds of fertilizer for the fields besides this human waste. America had taught her this and much more about her country that she had not known before. She liked America. Of course she did not think about that now. Her country was at war --- and with America! How odd it seemed! Ten years ago Americans had been so kind to her. She loved the broad green lawns, the white houses behind white picket fences, the shining white of the bathrooms and kitchens, the busy streets full of bright colored cars, and the gaudy five-and-ten-cent stores. She had visited the little town where Gaines Sensei was born. It was such a peaceful village. Gaines Sensei's friends and cousins had warm voices and their eyes were kind. Somehow she understood Gaines Sensei better after this, understood that as she grew older and sat so often with her hands quiet in her lap she was drawing up into her soul the peace of that Kentucky town. This must have been the secret of her calm in times of crisis. Just the thought of Gaines Sensei brought her courage for the day before her. Strange how the courage and the strength of people kept on growing in others after they were gone. That in itself was a kind of immortality.

If she could only understand this war. Five years ago when the foreign teachers left the school they had said there would be war, but none of those they left behind even half believed it. Now they knew what war was. They knew hunger. They knew cold without even the small heat of a charcoal brazier. They knew the deeper cold of fear at night when sirens shrieked and the fingers of search lights swept the sky. Last night as the sirens sounded she had rushed through the darkness to her place in the first aid station on the corner. For hours they had waited silently, and then with the all clear signal they had gone home again. The coldness of that fear followed her. But this she must not think about. Thinking of the more distant past was safer. Then there had been a sense of security that now seemed lost forever. False security perhaps it was, but at the time it had seemed a deep reality.

Thirty years had passed since she first came to the school. Things changed in 30 years. Hiroshima had changed. The streets were wider; all of them were paved. Street cars and buses crossed the city, east and west, north and south. There were tall, new buildings like Fukuya's, a department store. She had gone there only yesterday. She had watched the country people ride to the roof on the elevator, stand in awe as they looked down on the city spread beneath them, saunter down the broad staircases and view the merchandise, floor by floor. Down the street was the radio station and all those concrete bridges. Thirty years ago one crossed the rivers in small ferry boats.

The school had changed too. New buildings had been built, old buildings changed. Many of these changes she had seen. Others she had heard about. Sometimes nature all alone had brought the changes. Just as the first kindergarten building was finished a wind storm had blown it to the ground. But through Gaines Sensei's courage it had been rebuilt, larger than before. There had been a fire that destroyed Gaines Sensei's home and the main school building. The fire was remembered now not so much for the buildings it destroyed or for the buildings that came after it as for the picture of Gaines Sensei climbing through the window in her red flannel nightgown, her arms full of as many volumes of her new Encyclopedia Britannica as she could hold. What fun it had been to reproduce this scene at the numerous pageant parties in the dormitory. The dormitory was perhaps the most changed of all. With a dignity becoming its long years of service, it had held together through a long trek around the block, and had settled itself contentedly into the new soil of the college compound. There it stood this minute, its outside stuccoed, its insides turned around. Only those of long ago remembered the "old dormitory". Now it was the English building. Perhaps that was the reason she never really learned to speak English. It always seemed absurd to try to learn in the room where she and the three little girls she had roomed with had slept and played and talked of so many things outside of books. When the foreign teachers laughed at what they called her quaint expressions she forgave them, but she could not make them understand about the English building.

Yes, changes came, but always some things remained unchanged. These comforted her soul in times like now. The castle stood in the center of the city where it had always stood. The new city had not touched it except to fasten down its drawbridges and erect a modern building here and there within its grounds. Above them all stood the castle keeptower, apart from the hurry that surrounded it, scarred and old but never changing. Not all of the school had changed, there still was Sera Sensei. Mori San had met her yesterday crossing the high school compound. As long as she had known the school there had been Sera Sensei. She was as unchanging as the hills around the city or the island "Little Fuji" whose peak was always at the end of Flowing River Street as you walked toward the sea. Sera Sensei had the same trim little figure, the same quick step, the same gray hair combed smoothly back to a small knot on her head. Her dainty features were like carved old ivory, and her voice was always soft and sweet to hear. Seeing her yesterday had suddenly taken Mori San back to being a little girl on Sunday morning. The long line of children marched two by two across the playground, out the big front gate, around the corner, and down the long, long street to church with Sera Sensei at the head. Often it had been her lot to sit beside Sera Sensei. Sera Sensei always placed her sandals side by side beneath the bench and hid her feet quite neatly under her upon the cushioned seat. Her hands were folded motionless before her. Her back was straight, disdaining contact with the bench behind her. Mori San's feet always dangled. Her hands would not stay still. The sermon was too long for little girls, and the words were hard to understand.

There was an urge to look behind her, and something always itched. But there sat Sera Sensei, the perfect lady, and the little girl wanted to grow into a lady too. Sera Sensei taught them everything: the proper ceremonies for serving tea, the complicated art of flower arrangement, how to bow properly, and what to say and when to say it. She had been the mentor of their ways. Oh for a little of her calm and coolness for this day! Yesterday she had looked so frail. Mori San was startled with the thought, "Sera Sensei must be getting old.

Reluctant but determined, Mori San sat up and rose to meet the day. Already a strip of sunlight from the east window had crossed the hall and reached her door. Stooping, she gathered her pallet in her arms and carried it across the hall to the kitchen roof where she hung it on a bamboo pole to sun. Back in her room she began her morning toilet. Outside the window in the lilac tree the cicadas shrieked their strident warning of another scorching day. She looked at the lilac branches that brushed her screen. The leaves were brown and curling around the edges. They had never looked this way before. Perhaps it was too dry for anything to live. There had been no rains since the June rains ceased. Every day the radio warned about the low supply of city water. Do not water plants or gardens, they said. But something must be done about the lilac tree. She could not let it die. This morning Ojii San was to stop by on his way to work to look at it. If anything could save the tree Ojii San would be sure to know about it. She must hurry. He would be here soon.

Actually Ojii San was already there. He was sitting on the bench outside the kitchen door. A fig tree shaded him from the mounting sun. A white towel, twisted and tied in front, encircled his shaved head. His sun-browned face was creased into a thousand wrinkles and then into a thousand more as he smiled up at Yuki San as she came through the kitchen door, tea tray in hand. "Good morning, Ojii San," she greeted him. "I am glad that you could come. Mori San worries so about the garden. She will feel much better now that you are here. Let me get some of my salt-pickled plums for you to eat as you drink your tea. So good for you on a hot summer's morning." And off she hurried to the kitchen.

Ojii San sipped the tea with noisy relish. He laid aside his coolie coat and drew his pipe and a tobacco pouch out of his belt. Carefully he filled the small brass bowl at the end of the long pipe stem with a pinch of tobacco. He lit it and closed his eyes in satisfaction as a whiff of smoke arose. This had been a satisfying morning. His thoughts reached back to its beginning. Long before Mori San had begun to stir, Ojii San had been up. On summer mornings he demanded to be served whatever food there was to eat earlier than he did on other mornings. His wife, Obaa San, never dared to ask him why, and he never told her. On summer mornings he liked to take the castle road. It was a little longer, but it was cooler and quieter than the paved streets where the tram cars ran. Besides, he liked to walk. There were always things to think about at that time of the morning. Watching the sun rise on the castle had become a ritual for him. In the sun's first rays the dolphins on the tower shone dazzling white. Moment by moment the radiance spread, across the dark eaves, down the white walls. The cherry trees at the tower's base came alive and stood out bright and fresh against the deep, dark green of the pines and cryptomerias that not even the brightest summer sun could lighten. The long, dark tree branches stretched beyond the high stone wall, out over the waters of the moat. Night shadows still lingered where the waters gently touched the moss-green stones. Across the moat, weeping willows lined the dusty road where Ojii San always stopped. This morning the willow leaves had hung gray and heavy as if disheartened at the prospect of another day. Best of all he liked to listen for the popping of the lotus buds. At this time of the year the moat was full of great green leaves and swollen buds on slender stalks. In just five minutes this morning he counted at least a dozen pops as buds burst with that surprising sound. The bursting buds were his call to worship. There beside the moat as he faced the castle and the rising sun he bowed in slow and solemn reverence toward the East, toward Tokyo, the august dwelling place of Tenno Heika, His Imperial Majesty, the Emperor of Japan.

On this particular morning, as he bowed, his thoughts were troubled. Already at this early hour army officers, their swords clanking at their sides, hurried in and out of the great gates of the castle grounds. Now the gates stood open day and night. Ojii San had heard of war, he had even fought in war, but he had never known a war like this. There had been the old wars his grandfather had told him of so many years ago. Those had been wars fought when the castle was a fortress full of lords in shining armor. His grandfather and his great-grandfather had been a part of the old feudal system. They had served the lords who built this castle. How often in his boyhood he had stood in this spot and dreamed of arrows whizzing through the air around him, arrows shot from tiny slits that looked like black brush-pen strokes on the white surface of the castle walls.

He himself had fought when only a young boy in a short war with China. Ten years later he fought again against the Russians. He remembered well the day he stood with his companions within the castle grounds to hear the Emperor Meiji speak.

"Go!" the Emperor said. "Fight bravely for the honor of Japan."

All through those months of fighting they knew the Emperor himself was watching every battle and was sending out his orders from within the castle walls. He had fought in many battles under many famous men. The greatest of them all was the Battle of Mukden under the great leader, General Oyama. Afterwards they came home to flag-lined streets and the loud banzais of victory.

His sons too had fought. One in China and one in this war with America. How different this August was from that August 40 years ago when America had been the "go-between", arranging a peace conference in New England and helping Japan work out peace terms with the Russians.

Ojii San was too old to fight in this new war, but he had made his sacrifices. Five years ago his elder son died somewhere on the battle fields of China. This morning, on his way out of the house, he paused a moment with bowed head before the small white wooden box that held the ashes of his younger son, who was killed in the fighting on Okinawa. Two months ago he and the women of his household, his wife and his son's wife, went down to the city docks at Ujina. There they waited long hours in silence as the great white ship unloaded its white cargo, hundreds of small wooden boxes, each wrapped in a white cloth and carried by a khaki-clad soldier. Through the gloom of June rains they carried the white box home. Now it rested by the god-shelf in the corner of the best room in the house awaiting time for burial. Both sons were gone, but perhaps his loss would help bring victory. Through dying, his sons had brought new honor to the Emperor. What more could any father ask than this?

His sons were gone, but they had not left him entirely desolate. There was a grandson, Tajiro, now eight years old. Already he was learning what it meant to be a soldier. As Tajiro drank his tea this morning he said, "Ojii San, do you know where we go today? This is the day for our school to clean the grounds around the Soldier's Shrine. It will truly be hot work for you know there are no trees around the Shrine, but we can stand the heat when we are working for our country. Before I begin my work I shall go to the steps that lead into the sanctuary, and there I shall worship the spirit of my honorable father. Then I shall work with all my might for the glory and the honor of our Emperor."

"So you will honor the name of your house, my son," Ojii San had answered.

While they were talking the entrance bell jingled, the sliding paper door opened softly and Ayako San, Tajiro's mother, came in. She bowed her morning greeting.

"Ah, my honorable mother has returned," cried Tajiro. "Welcome home! Has the night's work tired you very much?"

"Thanks, my son, I am a little tired, perhaps. We are working with great speed just now. Weariness, however, does not matter if our guns have all the ammunition that they need. Some day we shall win this war, and then our weariness will end."

"Yes, we will win this war, if we do not all starve first!" complained Obaa San. "If only I could find the food you need to keep you strong for working! But what can anybody do with only chicken feed for rice, with no meat or fish, and only sweet potato vines and weeds for vegetables? Even Tajiro weighs ten pounds less than he weighed two months ago."

"Woman!" Ojii San chided. "You must not complain. Victory will come soon. In the meantime you have much to do. You spend too much time with those friends of yours at the bathhouse. And too much money too. You only go there for the gossip. I can take my bath in half the time you spend. You are only cross this morning because you did not sleep last night. The air-alert was long. The air-raid shelter is no place for sleep.".

There beneath the willows Ojii San pulled himself back to the present. He had stayed too long this morning, there was work to do. He gave one last glance to the castle. The sun shone full upon it, lighting it from top to ground. It seemed to him no longer of importance in itself. It was a symbol of the protection for which it had been made and nothing more. This thing called war had long outgrown it. Instead of power coming from inside the castle, as it had in days gone by, it now surrounded it, was even over it in the sky itself. But still the symbol stood.

The slamming of the screen door roused him. Yuki San had brought the plums.

"You will find these plums not fit to eat now that I have brought them. They have no taste at all. I am sure the ones Obaa San makes for you are far, far better. But try one anyway. It may help to keep you from feeling the heat so much."

Ojii San ate a plum and sipped his tea. "They are by far the most delicious plums I ever ate," he said with his one tooth gleaming as he smiled his thanks. "That worthless wife of mine must learn to make them better. She must ask you for your recipe."

"Mori San will be here as soon as she has eaten," said Yuki San. "Meals take so little time these days, she will not keep you waiting long. How your wife feeds four I cannot understand. We scarcely find enough to feed the two of us. This winter we shall starve. So many fields are lying idle with the men all gone to fight and the women in the war plants. Your Ayako San is working in a war plant, is she not? I suppose that Mori San would work too, if the secret police trusted her. Imagine following Mori San around! They have followed her, you know, since she came back from America. So foolish of them when she is the most quiet person in this town. But we were talking about food. You came through Hakushima. Was there any fish this morning? I haven't had a decent piece of fish since this war started."

"You women do too much complaining," Ojii San chided, pulling on his coat once more. He rose to the full height of his scant five feet and thus attained a dignity in spite of his absurdly crooked legs. "The Emperor does no complaining. Her Majesty, the Empress, gives constantly to feed the poor. There will soon be food for all. The American devils must come to their senses soon. Even now their greatest cities lie in ruins. You have heard and I have heard. Last night our patrol planes cleared the skies above Hiroshima. Soon we will drive them back across the ocean -- or into it."

"But Kure has been bombed three times!"

"With little damage. They soon will know, those foreign devils!" Ojii San washed his mouth out with cold tea.

Yuki San was still far from convinced. "Yesterday at the bath-house a woman said her husband picked up a printed paper in the street that said Hiroshima was doomed, that soon the bombs would fall here too. It said the only way to live was to get out. But where is there that we could go?"

"Idle bath-house gossip," growled the old man.

Mori San called from the house, "Come to the front, Ojii San, I will meet you there."

Yuki San led the way around the house into the garden. Mori San was standing by the lilac looking at its browning leaves. Ojii San went to stand beside her and the two became absorbed in garden talk. Yuki San grew tired of standing and sat down on the bench beneath the willow tree. She could not hear what the two beside the lilac tree were saying, but she knew that this was most important. She must not bother them.

It was important because this was no common lilac tree. Its top branches touched the roof, and in the spring they blossomed into a cloud of snowy white that filled the yard, the house, even the street with fragrance. As she looked at the tree from her shady spot, Yuki San remembered the day it was planted. This house was new then. Gaines Sensei and her sister, known to all as just Miss Rachel, moved their things here from Lantz Hall, across the college tennis courts. Yuki San moved her things with theirs. It was a day of great celebration. Graduates came from far and near. This was their house. They built it with their money and gave it to Gaines Sensei for her own until she died and then to Rachel Sensei. After Rachel Sensei was gone it was to be a home for Alumnae. The sisters had always wanted some place they could call their own. They called the house Gaines Hall.

As Yuki San remembered, it was just a few days after the big celebration that Gaines Sensei called her to the living room one morning. "We are to have a guest," she said. "She is coming all the way from Peking to see us in this new home of ours. The guest room must be cleaned and aired. Fill the house with flowers. This guest is an old and very dear friend of mine and we must make her welcome." The next day she arrived, a tiny, lively Chinese lady. Yuki San smiled now remembering all the packages she brought. They kept on coming, for days it seemed, large ones and small ones and in the most peculiar shapes. There was a long, narrow rosewood table with beautiful carved dragons on it to stand by the windows in the living room. There was a round, carved teakwood table for the center of the room. And then there was the lilac tree. How carefully they planted it, tended it and watched it grow. It was only a little tree, scarcely three feet tall, and now there stood Ojii San craning his neck to see the top.

Mori San was thinking too how tall the tree had grown in 15 years. It was nothing but a little bunch of sticks when they planted it. The roots looked quite lifeless as they put them in the ground. But they fertilized it, watered it, protected it. How eagerly they watched for the first faint signs of leaf buds on the stems. The gardener would water it and shake his head. "I think there is no life here," he would say.

"We shall wait a little longer," Gaines Sensei would answer. "It is new to our soil here. It will take a little time." The same thing Mori San often heard her say of girls who showed no promise. "Give her time. The soil is new. She will adjust herself and growth will come." Girls responded. The lilac responded, too. Buds formed, green leaves opened and the tree grew. Two years passed before the first white blossom appeared. Each year the tree grew a little taller, and each year brought more blossoms. Gaines Sensei died before the tree reached the second story windows. Then Miss Rachel took the lilac for her special care. Mori San could hear her now calling to the kindergarten children who sometimes came to play in the garden. "Don't touch the lilac tree," she would say. No other plant in the garden had been guarded with such care. But now Miss Rachel, too, was gone. If only Gaines Sensei and Miss Rachel could have seen the wealth of blossoms the tree had held this spring! Somehow, since the war began, the tree had come to mean much more to Mori San than it had ever meant before. It stood for all that Gaines Sensei and the school had given her. It was even more than that. It stood for all the things of beauty and of good the school had added to the lives of the girls schooled there during its 60 years. It stood for all the art, all the music, all the better living the school brought into Hiroshima. Like the lilac tree, its roots were deep; it could be counted on to bring forth flowers of beauty and its fragrance was for all. Yes, the lilac tree must live against all odds. So little that was beautiful remained to counteract the evil that engulfed them.

Ojii San turned, a dried leaf in his hand. "Without water the tree will die," he said.

From beneath the willow tree Yuki San responded, "We will see that it has water. Every night before they turn the water off I save a bucket full for my next day's scrubbing. Every night I shall use it to water the lilac tree. Gaines Sensei always said that I scrubbed too much anyway. Besides a bucket full of Mori San's bath water will serve as well to do my scrubbing. If the tree needs only water, we will not let it die."

"I shall dig a trench around the tree now," Ojii San said to Mori San. "Tomorrow on my way to work I shall bring some fertilizer I have saved. Then with a little water every day until September rains begin, I think that we can pull it through." Yuki San went with Ojii San to find the spade, and Mori San sat down upon the bench that Yuki San had left. The street beyond the wall was alive with an incessant clattering of wooden clogs, the slow creaking of well-loaded carts, the steady tapping of a blind man's stick close to the wall. From across the street on the high school grounds came the rhythmical counting for morning exercises -- ichi, ni, san, shi, go, roku, shichi, hachi -- one, two, three, four, five, six, seven, eight. The counting ceased. Then came the shouted command to face the east, the crunching sound of heels turning on hard earth, then silence. Mori San knew what the silence meant. The school was sending morning greetings to the Emperor in one long united bow.

3. First School Building located at Kaminagarekawa - 1890.

4. Reconstructed School Building after fire - 1892.

5. 400th anniversary of the Lord Asano family.

6. Hiroshima Girls' School students and Japanese faculty assemble on the school grounds to march toward Ujina and join others in welcome to Field Marshal Oyama from the Russo-Japanese War of 1904-1905. Miss Gaines was in the city to be presented to the Field Marshal with other notables. The other foreign teachers were with members of the Red Cross where they served in Military Hospitals.

7. A Jinrikisha - 1924

CHAPTER 2
THREE FRIENDS

Beyond the tea-olive hedge the street gate clicked and Yamada Sensei came into the garden. Mori San was always glad to see him. She watched him as he crossed the grass to sit beside her. It was hard to recognize in him the dumpy, jolly little man of more than 20 years ago. He came to the school straight from four years at Columbia University to be the sociology professor. The girls liked him. He was human, and he saw his students not as classes but as people. They liked his sense of humor and his frankness. Looking at him now, Mori San could see that he had aged 10 years in five. His plump figure had thinned out and in that terrible civilian uniform the government required all school teachers to wear he looked limp and discouraged. Even this early in the morning there was nothing fresh about him. How she hated the dirty shade of khaki in that uniform! Perhaps it was the cloth and not the shade that made it so impossible. Nothing made of fiber cloth could ever hold its shape or color. Only when she saw his face could she believe that all the dingy uniforms in the world could not make him a pessimist. His eyes and voice were full of an alertness and an optimism that one seldom met in these days.

She spoke to him. "Good morning, Sensei, you are out early."

"We are all out early every morning now," he said. "I am not used to school in August, but if we have to have it, it is better to come early and get through. Every morning I am up by five. The walk from home takes 50 minutes, and I try to be here by six-thirty."

"I should think you would be sorry you moved so far away. You always lived so close to school. If we had only known how long this war would be you might have stayed in town and saved yourself that walk these summer mornings."

"No, that is one thing I shall not be sorry for. Some day you will live there too. It is beautiful. Every day I climb the hill and walk along the ridge under the tall pines. Always I keep saying to myself, 'This is Ushita Yama. Someday we shall build our new school on this mountain!' You know, one needs a hope like that in times like these. As I stand on the highest knoll I set each building in its place - the high school, college, auditorium, gymnasium and dormitories. The paths beneath the pines are filled with girls who seek for learning, and their eyes are free from fear. On the hillside to my right stands the music building that looks so beautiful in the blueprints we keep locked up in the college safe. In the minutes that I stand there, I forget there is a war. My imaginings run riot, and I see great stores of things, materials to build with, equipment for our classrooms and our laboratories, books for the library, pianos, tennis courts----"

Mori San laughed, "Sensei, you sound as Moses must have sounded on Mount Pisgah when he looked into the promised land. All this is very far away, if it ever happens now. All the land here and these buildings must be sold. There isn't much here we could use in a new school, only a few pianos and the books. We are too busy with the needs of every day to look so far into the future."

"You look too much at what there is today. When we bought that mountain we were wise. Some day there will be a school built on it. In the meantime, I am glad to have my house already built in that pleasant valley where each day I can lay new hold on hope. Some day we shall take Gaines Hall and you and the white lilac tree and transplant you on that hillside. You will be surprised how the fresh air will bring new life and energy," Yamada Sensei poured his enthusiasm on her.

Mori San replied, "My thoughts keep running on the past instead of on the future. This morning I have lived through years that went by long ago. My thoughts have made me feel so very old. To me the past seems safer. I can see so little hope for things to come."

"You should have some work to keep you busy," he said. "The kindergartens should have opened on the first of August too. Then by this time in the morning you would be half way across the city with the present pressing down so close upon you that the past and the future would be forced out. Thirty kindergarten children can keep your mind from wandering far."

Mori San's face clouded as Yamada Sensei spoke. "There is so much sickness now among the children that their parents are afraid to let them come together. Just yesterday I went to the funeral of one of my little boys. He was always such a happy little fellow. It was hard to see him dead. Perhaps it was the crematory that depressed me so. There were five funerals being held while we were there, and others still were coming in the gates as we were going out. And that was only one of all the crematories in the city. As I came home my ears kept ringing with the droning voices of the priests as they intoned the services. Intermingled was the tinkling of the service bells that I could hear long after I was home again. And now, just thinking of it, I can smell the incense that was rising here and there where priests were kneeling. The grounds were full of incense as it hung stationary in the hot, quiet air."

"You should be used to death after eight years of war," said Yamada Sensei with a quick look at the woman by his side. "But let me give you something else to think about. Your speaking of the past reminds me of what I came to talk about. I think you graduates should make some plans for the old piano in the Gym. As an officer of the Alumnae Association, you can bring it up at the next meeting. That piano has seen service long enough. It will be completely ruined with the constant banging that it takes. It would be hard for high school girls to understand its value when it looks the way it does. I think the time has come to put it in some place of honor with a card attached saying: 'This is the first piano that ever came into the city of Hiroshima.'"

Mori San said smiling, "Some one really should write its story. It has had a most exciting life. I used to love to hear Gaines Sensei tell us how they dropped it in the sea when they unloaded it at Ujina. Imagine how those workmen must have felt when they saw it going down into the water."

"Gaines Sensei must have shuddered when she saw it going down," Yamada Sensei laughed. "I think the best part of the story comes after they had fished it out again. It must have taken days to get it into shape again, but finally they got it here. Do you remember how they said the men who brought it set it down where they were told and then stepped back three steps and bowed before it with great reverence because they thought it was the god-shelf of the foreign ladies? That scene would have been worth seeing. Yes, the piano has a history that should be written and preserved."

"Hata San is coming by this morning, and I shall talk to her about it. We will see what can be done. It must be time for her to be here. She said that she was coming early."

"She will have to hurry to get here early now. It is already after seven, and time for me to go. My classes had to go to Ujina to meet a sick-ship coming in. I have taken them so often that they let me off this morning. I am going home to do a little digging in my garden. We want you to come out to see us. It has been so long since you were there. We have some cabbage that is growing well. Maybe we could even feed you! Oh, for the old days and a cup of coffee! With sugar and with cream! I think I miss my coffee as much as I miss white rice. But now who is thinking of the past?" He rose to go. "Bring Hata San and walk out to Ushita tonight. It will be good for both of you." By this time he was already half way to the gate. He waved goodbye and disappeared into the street.

"Mori San," Ojii San called as he stepped out from behind the lilac tree, "there is nothing else that I can do this morning, and it is time for me to go to work. I shall come by again tomorrow morning. Remind Yuki San about the water." His gnarled hand swept the towel off his head. "Sayonara, Good day to you," and he bent in a quick, low bow.

After he had gone, Mori San turned and went in through the sun porch for another cup of tea. From the kitchen window she saw Yuki San and the old woman from the green grocer's just across the bridge sitting together on the bench in the shade of the fig tree. Their voices were as shrill and as incessant as the continuous murmur of the cicadas that seemed to grow more strident as the day advanced. She made her tea and sat down weary at the kitchen table. Hata San would want some tea before they started on the long hot walk to Hijiyama.

In the yard the old woman had taken her bamboo basket from her back and was cooling her hot face with a damp towel. There was very little in her basket, a few stalks of lotus root, a few mountain potatoes, some wilted sweet potato vines, some sun-dried seaweed. Yuki San had bought a stalk of lotus root and a little seaweed, and now sat listening to the old woman's story of the morning.

"My father taught me long ago that it was good to offer daily prayers before the gods. I remember, when I was very young, being wakened very early in the mornings by my father's clapping hands as he worshiped at the household shrine that he had built in a corner of our garden. Many times he took me with him to the big temple by the river. When I was married all those years ago, I was young and frightened. I remember what my father said about the gods. Since the day I left his house I have always said my prayers before the temples and the shrines. Since my son went to war I go each morning, very early in the first gray light of dawn. There is no other time. Nigitsu is near, you know, and so I start my praying there." She stopped to sip her tea.

"These are days that make one think of praying," said Yuki San. "Last night, long after midnight, I heard the beating of the hand drums of the Nichirens. They passed beneath my window, looking ghostly in their white robes against the blackness of the night. I think there were five of them. It is strange to hear them in the summer time. Mori San says that Central

Methodist down on Flowing River Street stays open day and night for those who wish to pray. Mori San goes often. And when I walk down Banner Street and pass the Catholic compound, there is always someone kneeling before the statue of the lady in the garden. Mori San says Catholics pray to her."

"Yes, it is a good thing, praying," the old woman answered. "This morning when I reached Nigitsu the stone walk between the cryptomerias leading to the inner shrine was still quite dark. When I stepped into the inner court the birds in the big camphor tree began to twitter noisily. I heard them twitter that way once when a long black snake crept toward them across the steep roof of the shrine. I pulled the bell rope. The gods must wake to listen. I threw two pennies into the money box. The gods hear best when paid. I knelt a moment on the topmost step and asked the gods to keep my son safe for today."

She told the next part of her story quickly. In the growing light she had gone into the street again, out through the big red gate where the prayer bespattered demon guardians frowned down upon her. The pigeons rose, she said, in startled flight as they heard the clatter of her wooden clogs upon the stones.

"I never liked that gate," said Yuki San. "Those wooden figures with those wads of chewed white paper stuck all over them always look so dirty, and the pigeons do not make them any cleaner."

The old woman did not respond. In her mind, she was walking on a road beneath the pines that held the shadows of the night in their dark branches. "You know the road that leads to the East Parade Ground and is lined with shrines and temples. I always pray before them all. Some people say that praying to the Shinto gods or to the Buddhist gods alone is quite enough. To me it seems far better to offer prayers to all of them. Some one of them may listen when I pray.... Have you seen the lilies in the pond before the small shrine just beyond Nigitsu? Early in the morning they are beautiful."

Yuki San poured hot tea in the cups. They drank together for a moment, both silent. Again the old woman was not there. She was walking over water-lilies on a curved stone bridge beneath a high arched torii to the shrine within. Again she clapped her hands three times and bowed in reverence to the gods enshrined there.

She set her cup down on the bench and spoke. "I stopped long enough this morning to look closely at the great Imari Lantern that stands before the shrine. Its blues and reds and golds were brilliant in the sunrise. It reminded me of Gaines Sensei's Imari candle sticks you showed me when I helped you clean."

"They say," said Yuki San, "that some Korean King sent it long ago to be placed before the shrine. I always wonder how they got it there and set it up without its being broken."

"It was so calm and peaceful there this morning that I wanted to sit down on the stone bench underneath the gnarled pine tree and look forever at the lilies and the trees."

"But it would not have stayed that way," Yuki San reminded her. "In just a little while the street would have been full of soldiers from the barracks just across the road. Many other people would have come to worship at the shrine."

"Yes, I know," said the old woman, "and besides I had to finish with my praying and be home again before the sun was too high in the sky. But after I leave the little shrine I always climb the long stone steps up to the little Buddhist temple that hides itself in the trees against the hillside. You remember, the one that looks out on the east parade ground. I am always out of breath before I reach the gate. I stopped this morning and sat down for a minute on the last step just beneath the wooden gate. Then I went into the courtyard where I said my prayers again. I must have awaken the birds there, too. They twittered all around me."

Yuki San spoke slowly. "I think that is the temple that belonged to Sera Sensei's family."

"The Sera Sensei in the high school dormitory?" asked the old woman quickly.

"Of course, <u>our</u> Sera Sensei," Yuki San replied.

"Tomorrow when I go I shall feel much more at home there," laughed the old woman. "Sera Sensei is a friend of mine."

"In the mornings when you go to pray do you climb Inari Yama?" asked Yuki San, amused.

"Of course I climb Inari Yama. At the little Buddhist temple I am already one-third up the mountain. The climb from there is steep but not so long. I go out the side gate of the temple and up the path roofed over with hundreds of red torii. They arch the path right to the top. I wonder every day how people find the space to put in new ones, but now and then another one appears."

"Inari Yama, sacred to the gods of grain," said Yuki San. "Do you really think that you will have more rice to eat this winter because you walk devoutly underneath those torii every morning, because you stop to bow before the fox shrines set along the way? Why fox shrines anyway, I wonder? Why should grain gods choose to live in foxes? These Christians that I see and live with say that God does not dwell in such shapes and images. They say he is a spirit and you feel him in the air and see him in the trees and flowers around you. I do not know."

"I may not have more rice, and then I may. There are others besides me who pray there. This morning I met men coming down from worship at the big shrine as I was going up. At one fox shrine a woman knelt. She was still there when I came down, quiet as the stone fox image at her side. A girl set offerings of rice before another shrine. I know that it is good to worship and believe. Perhaps it is the Christian god that speaks to me when I have bowed at all the shrines and sit resting on the mountain top. I say my last prayers there. The beating of the drums and the chanting of the priests at morning service in the big shrine fill the mountain top. From my place upon the stone behind the shrine I look down on the gray roofs of the city. Always there I find a quietness of spirit. It gives me strength to go on with the day. Perhaps it is the Christian god that speaks."

"I do not know," Yuki San repeated.

"This morning when I reached the stone there was another woman there. She sat beside me, near enough for me to touch. We did not speak. I do not think she knew that I was there. I do not know what gods she prayed to, but I am sure she prayed. There was something close to us that seemed to bring our souls together. I left her there when I came down...." The old woman paused, then spoke again.

"I wish that I could tell you how the city looks and how it makes me feel when I sit there on the mountain in the mornings. It spreads out beneath me like a giant's hand. I can see five of its rivers. Five bridges I see that cross the river nearest to Inari Yama before the waters pour themselves into the sea. Just beyond Sakai Bridge I see our boathouse. It looks so small I wonder how the two of us can live there. The rivers look so shining and clean. And yet I know there is brackish water in them. The railway station with its tracks that gleam bright in the sun seems a quiet peaceful place. I know that people see inside it, pushing one another, crowding at its gates. Inside its walls there is no peace. Beyond the station the green of Hijiyama makes an island halfway between Inari Yama and the sea. I know that one whole side of that green island is covered with the white of marble tombstones. Far to my right the castle keep-tower rises white and clear against the sky, more like a picture than a building that is real. And yet I know that all around it is the awful, tense confusion of another day of war. A floor of gray roofs stretches beneath me, crossed by streets that look like white chalk marks on the gray. I know that underneath those roofs live 300,000 men and women, good and bad. The good ones dream and work hard for their families and their country; the bad ones lie and cheat and lust. And so each day I look down on the city and I find her full of peace. But when I have come down again, I am a part of the seething, boiling soul of her, and in that soul there is no rest, no peace. ...I think that I feel sorry for a city that breeds war."

"Some morning I shall climb the mountain with you," said Yuki San.

"You would find it pleasant," the old woman answered, rising. "I have sat too long with you this morning, but I have enjoyed our talking here together. I feel quite rested now. I hope that you will let me come again. It is seldom that one finds a friend to listen to the things one wants to say."

"I am often very lonely. Mori San is seldom here. I am always glad to have some one to talk to," Yuki San replied. "If your husband catches any fish he wants to sell, we always want to buy them. Shall I see you at the bath-house at the usual time tonight? What a blessing bathing is in this hot weather!"

"Yes, isn't it? Sayonara, Konban made -- goodbye until tonight," and the old woman disappeared around the corner. Yuki San watched until she was out of sight, and then returned to her work inside the house.

From the kitchen Yuki San heard voices in the living room. "Hata San has come," she thought, "I must make some fresh tea." This done she hurried in to say good morning. To her surprise she found not only Mori San and Hata San but Kihara San as well. These three - Mori San, Hata San and Kihara San - had gone to school together. For 15 years their homes had been not more than three blocks apart. Almost every day they saw each other. The bond between them was a strange one for three women in such different circumstances. The school was the one thing they had in common, but that was a bond strong enough to keep them close to one another.

Mori San, unlike the other two, had never married. When chances came there were always things that seemed of more importance to her. For one thing there had always been Miss Rachel. Mori San was still in high school when word came to Gaines Sensei that her only sister, Rachel, had been injured in a fall. Her right leg was crushed and the doctors thought she might never walk again. Gaines Sensei left the school for one whole year. And then one day she was back again. With her was Miss Rachel on a stretcher. Mori San remembered how she and the other dormitory girls had stood in awe and watched as the men carried the sick lady from the street into the house. Then one day Gaines Sensei called her to her house. She took her to the sick lady's room and said, "Mori San, this is my sister Rachel. From today on she is to be your special charge. You will no longer do any work for me. You will always come straight from school to Rachel Sensei's room. She will tell you what she has for you to do. You must do everything you can to make her stay with us more comfortable."

These two had come to love each other very much. In following years Miss Rachel called Mori San her daughter, and Mori San cared for Miss Rachel as if she was the mother she lost when a small child. With careful nursing, Miss Rachel learned to walk again. Soon she was teaching English in two different schools. Through the 20 years she taught, many students came to know her and to love her.

One day, when Mori San had finished college, Gaines Sensei sent for her. "Mori San," she said, "you have finished your education. You have been a daughter to my sister. She appreciates the things that you have done for her, and so do I. Now the time has come for you to go. Every woman needs her own home. You should marry now and have your children. If you are ready, I shall speak to your brother, and we shall try to find a husband suitable for you."

Mori San replied, "I see no cause for hurry. I am content to wait awhile." And so the years had passed. From time to time kind friends would turn matchmakers and point out men whose virtues they extolled. Mori San would listen and sometimes she would look, but always she came to the decision that life was best just as it was.

For Kihara San there had been no choice but marriage. The only child of wealthy parents, it became her duty to produce an heir. The most important thing in life for any man was to have a son to bear his name. If no son was born to him but only daughters, then a husband must be found for the oldest daughter as soon as she was old enough to marry. Such a husband was a "yoshi"; he was legally adopted into his wife's family and took her name. When a son was born, he took the family name and became the heir to all the family wealth. A "yoshi" had been chosen for Kihara San before she finished high school. She had been married and had borne a son. Her father then died an old man, happy in the knowledge that a splendid grandson carried on for him and that his name was not without honor nor his wealth without an heir.

Kihara San lived on the street next to the school in the great house that her father's wealth had built. From the street only the gray tiled roof was visible behind the high tile-crested wall. All day the great wooden gate stood open, but even through the gate the passer-by could see nothing more than a well kept entrance court with formal shrubs around its inner walls and a flagstone walk that led to the wide front door. The spreading rooms of the house and its broad gardens were hidden from the common eye. Only a few chosen friends were invited in beyond the entrance court to share what lay within. Mori San and Hata San were of the chosen few. They had enjoyed the house on many a cold winter evening. The best evenings were those long ago before the war. Kihara San would come by in the morning, or sometimes in the late afternoon. She would say, "Tonight we have fresh lobster from Miyajima. Bring Hata San and come and help us eat it." Or, "Today delicious fish came from Onomichi. You must come for dinner." Sometimes there were Hiroshima fresh oysters that were very hard to get because merchants shipped them all to Tokyo; sometimes a special kind of bean or fish cake that Kihara San knew her two friends liked particularly well.

On these nights the Kihara's house was warm and glowing. The mat-covered floors were spread with thick, warm-colored Chinese rugs. There were red-lacquered Foochow screens, deep carved camphor chests, dark lacquered tables, rich brocades and priceless paintings on rich rolls of silk. The house was filled with Chinese treasures, for the Kihara money was made in Shanghai when the old Kihara was a merchant there. The dining room was almost filled with a high carved European sideboard that was always decorated with the most exotic liquors in bottles, large and small; liquors of all colors and many vintages. Facing the sideboard across the long, low table and the thick, silk cushions used for chairs was the latest model of a Westinghouse refrigerator, a true luxury, that only the richest could afford.

In spite of the luxury that surrounded her, Kihara San was a lonely woman. Her husband worked at the bank in the mornings and spent his afternoons out on the golf course. In the evenings, if he came home for dinner, he would drink himself into a stupor with glass after glass of golden heated saki before he ate his evening meal. More often he did not come home, and then she knew that he was drinking somewhere in a restaurant with a geisha by his side. When he came home at two or three in the morning almost too drunk to find the door, she knew that he had been for hours in the geisha houses she had seen on the broad side streets in the center of the city just off Flowing River Street. She had never seen inside the houses. She only knew that her father's money poured steadily into at least one of them. Sometimes she tried to stop him for their son's sake. It did no good for he never listened. She was just a woman and had no right to criticize the way a man arranged his world.

Sa-chan, her son, was her greatest joy. He had always been a good boy, and his rearing was more a pleasure than a task. On some long winter evenings when Mori San and Hata San came for dinner, they would take out the picture albums after the meal was over and spend hours going through the years of Sa-chan's life. Sa-chan would be fast asleep in his room, or as he grew older he would be sitting with his school books on the desk before him, lost to the world around him. The three women, heads close together above the album lying open on the table, became absorbed in each picture as it came. Here was Sa-chan, a tiny baby in his nurse's arms. Only his small head was visible above the long black ceremonial robe that shrouded him. He was on his way to the Shinto shrine for the blessing of the priest. How proud his grandfather had been that day! Here he was on the fifth of May when he was four years old. It was the day of the Boy's Festival. How straight he sat in that medieval armor in front of his Boy's Festival display! He was five in this one taken in the Shinto robes. There had been a ceremony for the dedication of the tea house in the garden on that day. Here was one taken on his first day in school. And one with Miss Rachel in the living room at Gaines Hall. He had his English reader in his hand. Here he was at his music lesson in the piano studio at the school. And another with a violin in his hands and Petroff Sensei by his side. So many more -- in races at the primary school, in his fencing garb, at jiujitsu practice, with his high school classmates in his military uniform. And now the newest ones of all -- Sa-chan in his soldier's uniform, first in training, then on ship board, then from some South Pacific Island, nobody knew just where. The years had been such short ones. He was only sixteen now. So young to be a soldier and so far away from home.

Since Sa-chan went away Kihara San was more lonely than she had ever been before. Having more friends would make things easier for her, but making friends was difficult for people of her class. She had too much money to make friends easily among the ordinary folk. And yet the Kiharas were not of the moneyed aristocracy - they belonged to the Narikin, the New-Rich class - and there was no mixing with the aristocracy. It was no wonder that Kihara San cherished these old school friends and found in them an outlet for her pent up soul. They were the only comfort of her days.

Last night Mori San told her that she and Hata San were going up to Hijiyama very early in the morning to see about the plants they had set out around Gaines Sensei's grave. This morning she had been up before the sun, picking flowers in her garden. Flowers were hard to find in flower shops in the city since the rains had stopped. She could not go with her friends to Hijiyama, but she could send the best she had.

Hata San, too, had been married. It was long ago when she was very young, just out of high school. Her husband was an army officer and her father was delighted with the match he had arranged for this his eldest daughter. On her wedding day she had gone away to her husband's house, to a husband she had not seen before that day, to a husband who was older than she was. Her husband put her in the care of his old mother. Hata San had tried to do the things expected of a new daughter-in-law. She cooked and sewed and scrubbed and washed and swept. There were seven in the family besides the bride and groom. It was her place to rise first and to spend the day in saving steps for her new mother. She had done her best, but it had not been good enough. Her new mother found her lacking. Her husband acted on his privilege as a new husband and sent her back to her father's house within a month after the marriage. Unless forced to, Hata San never thought of those days now. She had taken up her life where she left it. It had been much easier to wait on her own invalid mother through the years than to wait on the whole family of a husband whom she did not love.

For many years now Hata San had lived in a modest house a block beyond the school on Flowing River Street. She had never seen her husband after the day he sent her home. Through the years when her brothers had grown anxious and urged another husband, she always found excuses. Life as she was living it brought satisfactions. She did not want to change. When her brother's wife died in childbirth, Hata San had taken the baby girl and brought her up as her own. To support herself, her mother and the baby, she worked as office secretary at the school. For 10 years now she had been Alumnae secretary. She knew more about the girls - when they graduated, where they lived, whom they married, how many children had been born to them, whether they were rich or poor, and a hundred other things - than anyone had ever known before. She had instigated the fund used to build Gaines Hall. She had the energy it takes to get things done. Mi-chan, the little girl she had taken in, graduated from the school three years ago. A marriage was arranged soon after and Mi-chan had gone to a new home. Now she was back home again with her two children because her husband had been called to war. Hata San was glad to have her. She had been so very lonely since her mother died. She only hoped she could find enough food for the children. It was growing harder every day.

Hata San had spent much time here in this living room at Gaines Hall. The house was like a second home to her. She liked the quiet things Gaines Sensei always kept about her - the picture hanging above the mantle titled "The First Music Lesson;" the figure of the Buddhist goddess of mercy standing on the mantle with her green robes wrapped around her, her face a quiet benediction; the old Kutani bowl on the teakwood table; the Chinese rugs on the polished floors. It was comfortable and cool, even on this August morning. It was always hard to leave it, but the hours would not stand still. It must be almost seven. It would take an hour to walk to Hijiyama.

"Mori San," she said after finishing the tea that Yuki San had brought, "I think we should be going. Kihara San, you are going to the hospital to work this afternoon? Come by for me, and we can go together. I wonder if there would be time to go to Kondo San's when we have finished? You know that she had notice yesterday that her son was killed in action? Poor woman, and it has not yet been a year since her son-in-law was killed."

"She seems so brave," said Kihara San. "I know that I could never keep on going as she does if Sa-chan should be killed." She shuddered as if a cold wind touched her.

Mori San rose and called to Yuki San. Then she said, "We all should go to Kondo San's, she would be good for us. My own morale needs boosting. I have been feeling sorry for myself all morning. I think a talk with Kondo San would make me very much ashamed." Yuki San had entered. "Yuki San, we should be back by lunch time. Kihara San, if you are going home, we will walk that far with you." The screen door closed on the three of them as they went out together.

CHAPTER 3
TRIP TO USHITA

Yamada Sensei sighed as he said goodbye to Mori San and went out through the garden gate. It was a long walk to Ushita, and the sun was hot. But then, there was no hurry. He would take his time. He would have to wait till evening anyway to get his work done in the garden. The sun was too high now. He would go home through Hakushima. There was more shade that way. He was glad he had no classes today. Teaching seemed so futile now. Studies were the last thing that students thought about. This was not their fault, of course. How could they keep their minds on books? They sewed for army hospitals. They went to railway stations and docks to send the soldiers off and then to see them home again. They marched to shrines in honor of the dead. They leveled ground for new shrines. They even swept the city streets. He hoped those children playing in the street just ahead of him would have a fairer chance to learn than the present generation had. He reached the children and stopped beside them for a moment to watch them at their play. The game was hop-scotch. Fifty years fell from him. He was the size of this small boy who stooped to mark the concrete of the street with chalk. There was no chalk nor concrete in that long ago, only the hard wet sand upon the beach. His hands still held the feel of the broken shell used to mark big squares in the sand. "Jan-ken-pon," the small boy shouted. The children gathered round him, small hands extended. Yamada Sensei's big hand joined the small ones. "Jan-ken-pon," shrill voices chanted. "Jan-ken-pon," Yamada Sensei's deep bass rumbled. This time the hands were counted; the open hand was the sheet of paper, the tight closed fist the stone, and two hands, one large and one small with two fingers open, formed the scissors. No one won. "Mata, once again," Yamada Sensei shouted. Jan-ken-pon -- pon -- pon, feet stamping to the rhythm, jan-ken-pon -- each time the outstretched hands. Then two pairs of scissors and two sheets of paper; two winners, for the scissors cut the paper. Then again the winners shout the cry, "Jan-ken-pon" -- hands extended -- one large, one small. This time the big hand is a piece of paper, and the small hand is a stone. Yamada Sensei is the winner and must begin the game. He throws the stone, begins to hop on one foot, the other foot held high. The children shout with glee. But hopping is not easy after 50 years. Both feet touch the ground, again the children shout with laughter and Yamada Sensei steps aside. The children soon forget him in their ardor for the game. Yamada Sensei wondered, as he walked down the street, how many things had been decided by this "Jan-ken-pon" since it was first played centuries ago.

As he turned the corner into Hakushima, the street seemed full of little children. Some were playing tag in the shade of the big camphor tree beside the arsenal wall. A three year old was playing dolls, her house a square of matting spread upon the curbstone. She had some tiny dishes made of wood with maple leaves and sand for food. Two small boys poured dust from a gutter on each others heads with shouts of glee. An irate mother called from a latticed window and the boys ran guiltily away. Suddenly Yamada Sensei thought, "Why, all these children have been born since this war began. I wonder how much longer they must live before they come to know what normal life can be?"

The street was thronged with men and women on their way to work. They hung from steps of street cars rumbling past. They walked along the street in twos or threes, sometimes alone. They talked together as they walked or looked with eyes set straight before them, preoccupied, unheeding. What were they thinking of? The work they hurried to? The homes they had left? The days ahead of them? Were they content with what they had this summer morning? Were they hungry? Did they suffer? Were they all as calm and detached as they looked here in this street? Or were they thinking? Perhaps they moved automatically, going through the motions of another day. A horse-cart passed Yamada Sensei. The lean, hungry-looking horse was shaded from the sun by a small piece of canvas stretched over bamboo poles and fastened in the harness. His head was shaded by an old straw hat with holes cut in it for his ears to stick through. The driver did not ride but walked ahead, leading the horse by a rope tied to his bit. How foolish, yet how intriguing! "Sometimes," Yamada Sensei thought, "I am afraid that because of intense commercializing Japan has lost the quaintness that made up her charm." He liked the new things, but he liked the old things too. He hoped they would not all disappear.

His thoughts and steps were running parallel this morning. Here he was in front of what he called his curio shop. He called it his because he always stopped to see how the windows had changed since last he passed that way. The bronze tea-kettle was still there in the window on the right. It had been there now for months and he had stopped to look at it each time he passed. It was so straight and plain. The only decoration was a slender branch of plum embossed on it. The dealer said it had been made at least 400 years ago. He would step inside and ask the price again. Perhaps it was a little cheaper. Maybe he would buy it anyway. Few things today could bring such pleasure. Why keep on saving every thing he had for a tomorrow that he was not sure of? The entrance bell rang gently as he opened the shop door. The dealer came to meet him. Five minutes later he was on his way again, the kettle wrapped in newspapers swinging from his hand. What a foolish thing to carry through the streets on a hot summer morning! But his step was quicker and he smiled.

He crossed the bridge and turned onto the river road. He walked more slowly here in the cool shade of tall cryptomerias. He stopped a moment where the road curved with the river to look back down the river. A small sailboat loaded with white radishes, its sails as white as its white cargo, skimmed by him on the river. Above the red brick arsenal, the castle tower was white against the sky. Seeing it reminded him of the old book he had just finished reading once again. He found the book one night in a night stall down on Flowing River Street. It was one of those evenings in early fall when the whole city walked the streets to view the autumn moon. He walked with his wife and their young son to the nearest bridge where they stood to watch the moonlight on the water. It was late and the tide was in. The bridge was full of people watching the small boats floating like black swans on the river. The water was a shining mirror save where the oars disturbed it into silver ripples. They stood silent for awhile, looking on beyond the river to the outline of the mountains against the blue-green sky. Then they walked back together as far as Flowing River Street where his wife left him saying she must get the boy to bed. He walked on down into the city. Business had been good that night, and the street stalls were still open. He had known this before he reached them by the crowds that thronged the streets and by the smell of fresh roasting tea from the tea stall on the corner. He had not smelled tea like that for two years now, not since the city closed the night stalls. When he smelled it once again he would know the war was over, and life would be beginning once again. He walked on down the street, turned around and had started back again when he saw the book. An old man, as ancient as his wares, kept the stall. The evening breeze blew his thin white beard in sprays around him till he looked like the soap-stone figurine of the Chinese good luck fairy that stood in the center of his stall. Yamada Sensei stopped. He took the book up in his hands, touching it with care in order not to tear the brittle yellow pages. It was written on rice paper by the hand of some old scribe. As a specimen of brush-writing, it was a work of art. At first the artistry alone caught his eye. Then he read enough to see that it was an old chronicle of Hiroshima, just how old he could not tell. He asked the price and paid it gladly. Since that night he found in it an oft repeated joy. The castle always made him think of it because it told him how the castle came to be.

Four hundred years ago, the old book said, five small fishing villages had flourished on the land that now made up the city of Hiroshima. In 1589 Lord Mori, who held 10 provinces along the Inland Sea, decided to move his headquarters to this fertile delta land. In that same year, the building of the castle was begun. For four long years laborers by the tens of thousands cut the stones and hauled them into place for the foundations; cut the timbers and raised them into place to make the walls. By 1593 it was complete with moat, drawbridges, guard houses and iron-studded gates. Gradually the fishing villages had grown into a thriving feudal city which Lord Mori named Hiroshima - Hiro, meaning broad, from a kinsman, Hiromoto and shima, meaning island, from the name of a retainer, Fukushima, who had supervised the building of the castle. And so the city came to be called Hiroshima, the city of Broad Islands. The Lord Mori did not long enjoy his chosen seat. He was transferred to another fief and the Lord Fukushima took possession of his castle. From him it passed to the Lord Asano who maintained its feudal government up to the Restoration in 1868. Now only the walls, part of the moat, the five-storied tower-keep and a few gates remained. Various dwellings built by the nobles, sections of the city set aside for falcon mews and for horse pasturage and stables were all described in the old book. The section where the falcon mews had been still kept its name, Takajo Machi, meaning the street or section of the falcon tenders. Often when Yamada Sensei walked about through the old streets of the city he tried to see them as they must have been in the days of those first lords.

These lords had been devoted Buddhists. They used their energies and their workmen not only for building the castle and the city, but also for building huge Buddhist temples. From that time on the city was a Buddhist stronghold. As the city grew, more temples and more Buddhist schools were built. In the heart of the modern city were streets called the East and the West Temple Streets because of the many temples that stood side by side behind pine-shaded gates. In the business section of the city was a street made up of shops that sold nothing but things used by Buddhists. Yamada Sensei often walked along this street at night before the shops closed. The open doors revealed black lacquered butsu-dan, god-selves, with doors thrown wide to show the gleaming gold-leafed sanctuaries. The one electric light hung from the ceiling in each shop was reflected into many hundreds from the polished brass of candle sticks and incense burners set out on show tables and on shelves around the walls. The most beautiful candle sticks Yamada Sensei had ever seen were in the old, old temple near his house in Ushita. He was surprised to notice that he had almost reached the temple. There it was just in back of that enormous ginkgo tree. Since the time he had stopped for a minute to look back at the river and the castle, his thoughts had gone in one direction while his feet, through daily habit, had kept him on the road toward home.

He turned now from the river to the narrow path that led toward the hills. Here the houses thinned out. Women, working in rice fields here and there, stood knee-deep in black gummy mud, some with babies strapped upon their backs. How strange it was to see no men working in the fields. One old man patiently turned the water wheel, pumping water from the irrigation ditch onto the rice fields. His feet and legs moved rhythmically as if with each step he took he was mounting higher toward some far, invisible goal. He was, however, standing in one spot about four feet above the ground. He was held steady by a long bamboo pole which he grasped firmly in his hands. The other end was anchored in the ground. The steps he climbed did not take him upward but came round to him with each rotation of the wheel. His body was bare save for a loin cloth that he wore. His skin was tanned the color of the soil beneath him. Yamada Sensei wondered what he was thinking as he climbed those never ending stairs. Had he fought in wars long past, or had he lived through all his years close to the soil? Was he thinking now of the fall crops or of his grandsons fighting somewhere far away? Did he feel the heat on his browned body? Yamada Sensei felt the heat. He was glad that he was nearing home. He could see the Petroff's house ahead of him, which meant that within five minutes he would see his own, and then the long walk would be over for today.

A little farther on, Mr. Petroff greeted him. "Early you are coming from the city this hot morning. Is there no school today? Today I have only the house pupils. Tomorrow I must go to school again. I hope I do not miss a holiday."

"There is no holiday. My classes went to Ujina this morning. I took them last time so it was another teacher's turn to go today," Yamada Sensei answered. "Home is much more comfortable than any other place on days like this. 'Sumeba miyako,' as the proverb says, 'where you live, that is the capital'. I am sure that you find it much more pleasant living out here where there is more room to breathe than you found in the city. I often wonder why I did not move out sooner. It will be a great day when we get the school moved out here, too. Then you and I at least will have our work here close at hand and will not have to make this long walk every day."

"But we shall have to climb the mountain," answered Mr. Petroff. "It seems to me we lose one evil just to gain another."

"You should come sometimes and climb it with me now. Then you would be used to it when you have to climb it every day. The mountains that we climb every day soon cease to be so high, you know. The view from the top of Ushita Yama is delightful. It is good to have beauty to feed one's soul in days when it is hard to find the food we need to feed our bodies. Come sometime soon and bring Dannie with you. My son and I climb almost every day. We should be glad to have you with us. My best regards to Mrs. Petroff and to Sandra," said Yamada Sensei, bowing his farewell. He turned again toward home. He looked to see what time it was. Almost eight o'clock. If he hurried he would be in time to hear the news broadcast. Not that broadcasts ever said much these days, but it was a man's one point of contact with the world out there where things were going on. Always there was just a chance that something of importance might come through. He would give much to know the truth about this war. To him the government seemed nervous.

Through these last few weeks they had been too anxious to reassure the people. They even tried to minimize recent bombings. All the things they told were true, no doubt, but he wondered if they told the whole truth in the papers or on the radio. Perhaps it was as well. There wasn't much that could be done about it, but he would like a chance to form his own opinions. Yamada Sensei's thoughts turned back to Mr. Petroff. The man was far too thin. He must have lost as much as fifty pounds in those months after Pearl Harbor while they had him in internment camp. He looked better than he did when first released, but he still looked old and drawn. It had not been an easy thing to get him out of prison. Some of his fellow teachers at the school had worked long and hard in his behalf. He hoped Mr. Petroff would not ever need to know how much suspicion these kind friends of his had brought down upon their own heads because they spoke in his defense. The secret police would watch them all until the war was over. Now he and Mr. Petroff never talked about the war. One never knew when there were listening ears. Poor Mr. Petroff! It must be hard to live your life out as a White Russian refugee, a man without a country. But Mr. Petroff would not care for pity. He had a sense of humor and could make the best of things.

Yamada Sensei reached the last turn in the road. There was his house a little way ahead of him, looking comfortable and cool against the green background of the mountain. Where the path turned stood a stone image of the Buddhist Jizo San. Every time Yamada Sensei passed it he became a little boy again. He was walking on a path that looked across the sea. His grandmother walked beside him with his hand held tight in hers as they passed an ancient Jizo San beside the road. He could hear his grandmother's quiet voice. "Jizo San," she told him, "is the friend of all dead children. He is the guardian of their souls. Far away there is a river, Sai-no-kawara, to whose banks the souls of all good children go. There a terrible old witch takes away their clothing and gives to them a never-ending task. They must pile one stone upon another on the river bank until they have a pile high enough to reach to Paradise. Then as fast as stones are piled, the old witch tears them down. But Jizo San loves little children. If they pray to him before they die, Jizo San will come and drive the witch away so the little souls can reach their Paradise. He comforts children's souls and hides them safely in his great flowing sleeves."

Yamada Sensei stood looking down at the little image here beside another road. Its lap was piled with tiny stones. Around its neck hung layer upon layer of bright colored bibs, some faded, others new. He knew that each piece of cloth was placed there to clothe the soul of some dead child, and that each stone meant a prayer that the labor of some child's soul might be lightened. As he looked today Yamada Sensei thought of all the little children he had seen in the streets this morning with their lean and hungry faces. He wished that he might place a stone for each of them on Jizo's lap asking for the lifting of the burden of this war from their souls. With sadness in his heart he turned into his gate and disappeared into the shadow that was his front door.

CHAPTER 4
THE PETROFFS

From the gate, Mr. Petroff watched Yamada Sensei for a moment, then turned into the house. He settled himself as comfortably as the heat allowed in a wicker chair on the west veranda. The chair groaned and creaked beneath him, volubly asserting its great age. It sagged slightly to the left as another piece of wicker snapped in two, then wrapped itself in silent resignation. Mr. Petroff's eyes were closed. He seemed to doze, but always when he closed his eyes his mind became alert. Already he was far away with his sister in Harbin. For five years now he had heard nothing from her. He had not seen her since --- why, it must be more than 30 years! The way time passed astounded him. Over 50! Fifty-three he was on his last birthday. Anyway he felt his age, and 10 years more at least. Nothing like internment camps to put the years on one. These last four years had seemed like 10 at least. If this war went on much longer it would make an old man out of him. But it would stop. A war like this could not go on forever. He was sure that he saw signs of weakening in the Japanese. He was afraid to even think such thoughts as these. The infernal spying dogs of the gendarmerie seemed able to hear thoughts as well as words. Internment camp had taught him to keep his thoughts about this war deep down inside of him. Facts were facts, but thinking did not change them.

His sister. Thinking of her always took him back to the old Russia that had been his home. That world was like a dream world to him now. Only sometimes when he and his wife, Mariya, talked together of the old days did they come alive again.

This morning he was drifting back into the dream-world. It seemed unreal and far away. Image followed image in a quick succession. It had become more difficult as the years came and went to remember things as they had happened, one following the other. Certain things took precedence; others faded into dimness and were lost. This morning life began for him when he was 20.

He was just back from two years of study in a military school in Paris. Fortunately for him and his companions, their course had been completed before war was declared. There was the mad rush home, then the excitement and the gaiety of becoming a real part of the army of the Tsar of all the Russias. Then there was his wedding night. How beautiful Mariya had been! When he looked at her face, lined and thin as it was this morning, he could see it only as a mask behind which could be glimpsed the color and beauty of that night. He was 21; she 17. Happiness then, brief but complete. Then war, blood, terror. Surprise that the imperial Armies of the Russias could be defeated. And finally, flight. The bravery and fortitude of Mariya through those long days and nights had carried him through many hopeless hours since then. There was one narrow chance of escape from the Red Armies that drew closer with each hour. Some of his army friends had planned a slow retreat through uncleared forests and along untraveled roads across the border into Manchuria and on into Korea. He was asked to join them. He was the only one with family ties. He told them he must wait until he found a way to take Mariya out. Only the day before she had told him she was pregnant. He went home sad because he could not see the way ahead.

"Sergi," Mariya had said that night, "your friends have found a way and they are leaving. Is it not true?"

"Yes, my Mariya," he had answered, "but we too shall find a way." No rest she gave him until he told her of the plan. "But they have no assurance they will find a way out," he said.

"Get me a soldier's outfit just like yours," Mariya replied. "Go now and tell your friends that we shall meet them where they say."

After thought and much persuasion he at last consented, not because he felt they could escape but because it gave them time to work out something. If they stayed, there was no hope. There followed days of hiding and of sleeping in the dark and untrailed places of the forest; nights of stealthy walking along empty roads. Some of those with them died along the way. Some were discovered and dragged away to die. He and Mariya were lucky. With a few others they reached the border. How they crossed it he was not sure. He had stayed behind with Mariya until the way was cleared. He could still feel the surge of gratitude that came with knowing they were out of Russia. Nothing could ever be as bad again as those long weeks had been. Perhaps those days had made him calm when faced with Japanese internment. Mariya had sewn the family jewels into her uniform. Now for days they lived on what they brought, piece by piece. They exchanged jewelry for clothes at a pawnbroker's in northern Korea. They journeyed slowly on, moving ever south and east until the day they saw a sign in a store window. It was written first in Japanese, of which they knew nothing, and then in English, of which they knew little more. Finally they read enough between them to know that an orchestra needed a violin player. "But Sergi," Mariya exclaimed, "you play the violin." They searched the town for a pawnshop with a violin in it. Grandmother's emerald earrings were used to buy the violin. That was his first job outside of Russia.

The other members of the orchestra were Japanese. Their music could have been much better, but they were kind. They let Mariya travel with them and saw that she had a warm place to sleep and food to eat. The day came when they took ship with the traveling players. After two rough days, they landed at a city on the north shores of Honshu, the main island of Japan. This was a night that neither of them would forget, their first night in a Japanese hotel.

"Mariya," Mr. Petroff called from the veranda, "what fools we must have looked that night in the hotel."

Mariya's laugh rang out from inside the house. "What a thing to think about on a hot August morning! As if you had to go back more than 20 years to find enough to think about. Perhaps thinking of past troubles makes present troubles lighter. It is not always pleasant to remember times when one was foolish, but always I can laugh about that night in the hotel."

Mr. Petroff heard the sound of his wife's voice but not her words. He was lost in his own thoughts again. What happened on that night was one of his best stories. He loved to tell it to his friends. He liked to think about it because it always made him laugh, even when he was alone. It was late evening when the boat had docked. There was a short ride in a swaying ricksha through the growing dark, a quick turn into the lighted courtyard of the inn, the lowered shafts at the wide doorway and the smiling coolie waiting for his pay. The hotel keeper and a maid were kneeling just inside the entrance, their heads bowed to the floor. A porter took their shoes and set them neatly side by side on the stone doorstep, toes pointing out. Other maids appeared as if by magic and led them down the polished hall to sliding paper doors that led into a matting covered room. At once the maid brought tea. It was refreshing. Soon the evening meal was served in the same room on low red-lacquered tables. When they had finished, the tables were removed.

The journey on a rough sea had been hard for Mariya. The meal finished, she wished to rest. Although the room was large, there was no bed. "Sergi, where do we sleep?" Mariya questioned wearily.

"Perhaps in the next room," he answered, crossing to the sliding doors that made up one whole wall. Carefully he opened a door wide enough to look into the room beyond. Here was another room just like the one they were in. The only furniture was a low table in the center of the room. "We do not sleep in there," he told her turning back, perplexed. No one had told them that the maid would come when it was bedtime, take the sleeping mats down from the shelves behind the doors across the room and spread them on the floor to make their beds. But Sergi spied the doors and opened them. "Ah, here we are," he called with satisfaction, "two beds here in this closet. How very clever of them to hide their beds like this. Here are the mattresses."

With care he spread one mattress on the floor, the other on the wide shelf above. He lifted Mariya tenderly and placed her on the shelf. He took the bed upon the floor. They folded their clothes carefully and laid them on the bed so that the room would still look neat when they closed the closet doors. The beds were comfortable and they were soon asleep.

And then things happened that they knew nothing of till later. At ten o'clock the maid arrived to spread the beds upon the floor. She pushed aside the sliding door and looked into the room. She was aghast at the emptiness that met her eyes. What could have happened? She had brought the foreign man and his young wife into this room. She had brought them supper here. She had taken their empty trays away. No one had seen them leave the room, but there was no one in it! Frightened, she called the manager. Other maids heard and began to chatter. With the manager before them they all ran down the hall and thrust their heads excitedly into the empty room. The chattering increased as the guests in the hotel heard the noise and gathered around the door to see what happened. They crowded one against the other until the room was filled with clamor that grew louder with each moment. Then Sergi woke and thought, "What noise! the hotel must be on fire. Perhaps it would be best to find out what was going on." Sliding back the door, he thrust his head out. The audience he found was unexpected, but his surprise was nothing to compare with the amazement of the other people in the room. There was a quick, united gasp. Then guests began to disappear, convulsed with laughter. The maids tried to hide their giggles in their sleeves. The manager alone retained his usual composure and bowed his usual low bow. He motioned Mr. Petroff to come out from his seclusion. Then with his own hands he spread the mattress in its proper place upon the floor. Mariya by this time was standing with her robe drawn tight about her.

Her mattress was put down with proper care and they were left to finish out the night as it should have begun.

Mariya found her husband chuckling aloud when she came onto the veranda. She sat down on the stone step that led into the tiny landscaped garden and fanned herself with her kitchen apron. From the low azalea bush by the stone lantern, cicadas filled the air with shrillness. From the house, the piano sounded in the rich full music of the Franck Sonata. Their daughter, Sandra, was at her morning practice. Mr. Petroff sat up straight. He looked surprised.

"For a moment I had forgotten all about the children," he said, startled. Then standing above Mariya for a moment he placed his hand upon her head. "You know that you are very beautiful."

"Now I know that you are living in the past," Mariya laughed up at him. "I am glad, though, that you see me as I was and not as I am now. Sandra is expecting you. That Sonata is her call for you to come and practice with her. She has pupils at the school this afternoon. She is wise to get the practicing done early. I shall sit right here and listen to see if you have made improvement since the last time I heard you play together," and she pushed him gently toward the house.

Left alone, Mariya's thoughts began where Sergi's thoughts had stopped. Not long after the hotel episode Sandra was born. Mariya never lingered long in thinking of those days. They had been difficult. She had not planned to bring her first child into this kind of world. Her strength was long in coming back. Depression seized her often and stayed long. The little girl had grown, however, and Mariya had lost herself in the expanding personality of her daughter. Through the years she had forced herself into forgetting the strain of those first months in a new land. She remembered now the longing for security, the hope that some day there would be a place she could call home. It was a day in August, much like today when they had first seen the city of Hiroshima. They were still traveling with the orchestra. That night Sergi came back to the hotel and said, "I can get a job here at a picture show. It pays less than the orchestra is paying, but something better might come out of it." She remembered yet how grateful she had been. Life would be better now. The two years that followed were a nightmare to remember. One small cramped room for the three of them. No friends. The cold of that first winter in a Japanese house. No food but that she cooked in the room where they slept. And she had never cooked before. The discomfort of the Japanese kimono, but she had no other clothes and she could not sew. There was no money except for bare necessities. And then the day when she had known there was another baby coming. How miserable and frightened she had been! The months dragged on. She had made it difficult for Sergi. Again her time was near, and she was much more frightened than she was when they faced days and nights in the dark Russian forest. On one of her worst days, a foreign lady came. Miss Teale she said her name was. She was so tall she had to stoop to come into the room. She talked a great deal, but Mariya could understand little that she said. Sandra sat upon her lap and watched her with an evident delight. She went away, but the next day she was back again with two more foreign ladies. They said they were Miss Gaines and Mrs. Gray. Much later she learned that this was Gaines Sensei, as they called her at the school where she had taught for so long. Mrs. Gray was a Baptist missionary and lived in a big house near the Falcon Bridge.

The three Americans talked together for awhile that day in the English Mariya did not understand, and then Mrs. Gray said in the simplest Japanese, "I am taking the three of you home with me." Just by closing her eyes now Mariya could remember the quiet and the calm of that upstairs room. The clean smell. The crisp white curtains at the windows. Trees and green grass beyond. Here was peace. Three weeks later, in this clean bright room, her son was born. A Russian Greek Catholic baby in an American Baptist missionary's home! She loved to think of that. It made the world seem so much smaller and so much more comfortable. They called the baby Niki. Life changed for all of them when Niki came.

Many things happened quickly after this. Mrs. Gray said one morning, "You must learn to cook and sew." There were lessons in the kitchen and at the sewing machine. And she had learned. Sergi was asked to open a violin department at Miss Gaines' school. Mr. Gray found a house for them to rent. How beautiful the house had looked to her. Missionary attics were searched and the house furnished. She learned Japanese from her neighbors and English from the American ladies at the school. Sandra and Niki grew tall and strong. She and Sergi were very happy. Because Kobe had the nearest school for foreign children, Sandra was sent to Kobe when she was old enough to go. Soon, Niki too had gone. She and Sergi would have been very lonely if Dannie had not come. Another son, just when they needed him. What a pleasure he had been! She could hear him now, whistling as he worked on his new airplane.

It was good to have Sandra with them now through these uncertain years of war. If only they could hear from Niki!... The music in the house stopped. She had meant to listen to the Sonata. They liked for her to tell them where the rough places were. Her thoughts had carried her away. She had so many things to do this morning that she should not be sitting here thinking of the past. There was all the ironing to be done. But here was Sergi coming out to her again. She would wait.... He sat down on the step beside her and gave her a long look.

"It is Niki you are thinking of," he said softly. "I have a feeling we shall see Niki again before another year goes by. The war will end within the year. I am an army man. I know the signs. Remember the last letter Niki wrote? 'By the time this reaches you I shall be a real American. As soon as I have finished school and earned some money I shall send for you, and we shall all be good Americans together.' He'll do it, too. A few years more and he will send for us. Mariya, do you think that you will make a good American?"

"That letter came a long four years ago," Mariya answered, her voice dead.

"In a rich country like America, our son has maybe earned much money in four years. He will send for us, or he will come," Sergi assured her.

Again Mariya did not hear. She was standing on the dock in Kobe. Above her, on the deck of the great ship, stood Niki. The gangplank had been lowered; those yawning mouths in the ship's side that had swallowed all the cargo for this voyage were closed. Slowly the ship was edging out to sea. Sergi's arm had been around her, none too steady. There had been no tears, only a great thankfulness and a greater loneliness. Niki was on his way to freedom and a new home. If he had stayed a few months longer, he would have been drafted into the armies of the Japanese. He had been born here; he must fight here.

"Perhaps our Niki fights for the United States. He may be even nearer to us than we think," whispered Sergi. He dared not speak such things out loud. The ears of the Secret Police were long.

Secret Police. Why did he have to think about them? He shuddered with remembered terror of those days in 1941. He would always smell that prison and feel the cold of his damp cell. The awful food they gave them. The enforced silence. Hours and hours of questioning. He could see the stubby hands of Tanaka, the questioner, as he held the Big Book out before him or as he turned the pages slowly, one by one. The Big Book. A kind of Doomsday Book that held the record of the things he had done through days and months and years. Many of them little things that he did not remember doing. A trip that he had made in 1935. Where did he go? To Kobe was it not? What had been his business in Kobe on that day? He had called on Mr. Smith that day? What business did he have with Mr. Smith? Why had he lived at that American missionary's house? Why? Why? Why? Over and over again. Some days the same questions all over again and again. Some times his sense of humor helped him through. There was the day they asked him about other people who lived here in Hiroshima. There had been many Big Books on the table that day. In 1938-39, they asked, what kind of secret organization held meetings every Thursday night at the Presbyterian missionary house near Falcon Bridge? It must have been of great importance. Every Thursday night the same two ladies from Gaines Sensei's school rode down to Falcon Bridge at six o'clock or sometimes seven. They always came by taxi. Sometimes more of the ladies came. They stayed five hours or more. Petroff and his wife had been there sometimes, too. They must have known what those Americans were doing.

"Yes, I know what they were doing," Mr. Petroff said.

Black eyes glinted from across the pile of Big Books. Now. This was better. They were getting information after all this time. "Just what were they doing?" Tanaka asked again with satisfaction in his voice.

"They were having dinner," Mr. Petroff replied.

"What, having dinner until midnight? Come, come. You cannot play with us. What did they do when they had finished dinner? Come, we will have an answer!" Tanaka was roaring at him now.

"I think they always played some kind of card game. Rook, I think they called it. I am not sure."

"Card game? Rook? We do not know it. Do not lie to us. We can take care of those who lie! What do you mean? Rook! Bah!"

"The honorable gentlemen do not know Rook? I am surprised. I would suggest that the honorable gentlemen inform themselves. Not to know about it --- the famed and much respected gentlemen of the Secret Police Division! I am deeply shocked. There is nothing more that I can say to help the gentlemen." Mr. Petroff raised his chin a little higher and looked down upon his questioners from his lofty place above them. He had them nettled. He supposed they were still trying to find out just what had been the deep significance of those weekly Rook games. It gave him much satisfaction to see that he was able to disturb their peace of mind.

Well, that part of the war was over. They had finally released him. Of course they still watched every move he made, but he had gotten used to it. He even had pleasant talks with some of the men who followed him around. Soon it would be over. He knew the signs, as he told Mariya a little while ago. He had an idea that the Secret Police had a big surprise in store for them when this war was really over. He wanted to live long enough to see that look of arrogant superiority wiped off their ugly faces. He wished that one of those incendiary bombs that had been falling rather freely lately would drop right in the middle of Police Headquarters and burn the whole lot out.... No more of this. The clock was striking eight. He had a pupil coming. He must go in and get ready for him.

The chair creaked back into its normal shape as Mr. Petroff rose. He stooped to feel the soil around the little lilac bush that grew beside the step. The leaves were fresh and green, but the soil was dry. Dannie had perhaps forgotten that he was to water it. Tonight he would walk with him to the irrigation ditch and help him carry home some water. To Dannie the lilac bush was just another plant, but to Sergi and Mariya it was much more than that. It was a root from Gaines Sensei's white lilac tree. It had been a gift from Mori San when they moved into this house. This spring had brought its first white blossoms. To Sergi and Mariya it was a dear possession. With its blossoming each spring would come the memory of beauty they had known in other times and places; the memory of kindnesses of friends. It flowered with a quiet, calm simplicity, yet with a white shining radiance; so did the love they had, each for the other. It budded, leafed, flowered, grew in amazing, lush profusion; so did the children they had co-created. It was the sum of beauty they had known. It was the hope of beauty yet to come, a dear possession.

Behind the house Dannie whistled at his work. This airplane would be ready soon to add to all the others he had made. This one was his masterpiece. He must call his father out to see it. Best wait, though, until Tajiro brought the paper to him and he could get it pasted on. Then it would be finished. Tajiro San had promised to go by the paper store as he came home from school this afternoon. This was Monday; he should be here before four o'clock. Monday was the day he got home early. He hoped the money he had given to Tajiro San would be enough to buy the paper. He had given him the last sen out of his savings box. But it was worth it. Some day he might sell the plane for more than he put into it. If he could only get some rubber for the wheels. Maybe he could make some cardboard tires and paint them with black ink to look like rubber. That would keep him busy until Tajiro San came home. He hoped Tajiro would stop here before he went on to his own house. Obaa San always found so many things to keep Tajiro busy after he was home from school. But he was sure Tajiro San would hurry. Tonight they planned to test the plane. When he got to be as big as Niki, he would have a big plane all his own. Or, maybe, he would be a pilot of a clipper. He would want his plane to be all shining silver like the planes that Niki sent him pictures of one Christmas. How exciting it must be to feel your plane begin to climb the first time that you take it up. "I wonder," he said out loud to no one in particular, "how soon Dad and Mother will let me learn to fly."

Tajiro San was interested in these planes they made together, but he did not want to fly. He wanted to grow up to be a general in the army. Of course that was because his father had been killed while fighting in the army. Tajiro somehow felt he had to take his father's place. Tajiro was a "good guy". He had learned those words from Niki. Just before Niki left on the big ship that took him to America, he put his hand on Dannie's head and said, "Dannie, old boy, you are a good guy."

Tajiro was not like the other boys they played with. He was never mean or cruel. He was the best friend Dannie ever had. Some day when Niki took them to America he hoped Tajiro San could go along. It would be so lonely in America without him. Maybe they could go to the same college. Mother always said, "Dannie, some day you will go to college. You will be as big as Niki then." She always said this when she thought he did not want to study. Sandra taught him now. He supposed she was all right, as teachers go. He wished that he could go to school, though, with the other boys. After all, Sandra was only his big sister. When the war was over maybe they would let him go to school. There! That was all that he could do until Tajiro came and brought the paper. He would go out under the old camphor tree where it was shady and practice falling on his face the way Dad tried to teach him yesterday. Then he could show the fellows the next time they played air-raid.

While Dannie worked on airplanes in the Petroff's yard, Tajiro San was far across the city on the West Parade Ground. Since seven, he and all his classmates had been cleaning up around the Soldiers' Shrine. They worked in squads of ten; five swept the sun-dried sand, five carried trash away in bamboo baskets. Now and then they stopped to comment on the work they had done. "Ours looks much better than the other side," some one would say. "And look how much of ours is done!" Then back to work again, bamboo rakes and twig brooms raising clouds of sand dust all around them, bare backs shining wet and brown beneath the burning sun. Tajiro San had done as he said he would. He first had gone to stand bare-headed, arms straight at his sides, before the steps leading up into the shrine. His eyes looked straight ahead of him until they pierced the shadows of the inner shrine and came to rest upon the round metal mirror, made in the image of the sun, sacred, as he knew, to the great ancestress of his people - Amaterasa-o-mi-kami, the illustrious sun goddess. He bent in a deep, slow bow. Then he bowed again to honor all the soldiers whose souls were here enshrined. He bowed a third time, remembering his honored father and the words he had spoken to him, "My son, be brave. Honor your ancestors. Serve the Emperor." Rising, his eyes sought once again the gleaming mirror. Then he turned and, marching soldier-like, joined his companions at their work.

Of all the places the school was sent to work, Tajiro liked this place the best. There was so much here to see. A wide road cut across the Parade Ground just in front of the Soldiers' Shrine. All day long it was a busy road because it led through the great castle gates to Army headquarters within. This morning it seemed busier than ever. Big army trucks and cars rolled by.

Within the cars rode army officers who glittered with rows and rows of medals on their breasts. As each car passed the Shrine, each stiff back was bent in reverence. Tajiro swelled with pride. He too had bowed before the shrine this morning. When he was old enough, he would be a soldier. He might even be a general and have a car to ride in. Then he, too, would sit up straight, lean on his sword and frown as the general had done who passed just now. He would wear a moustache like one who passed by in another car a little while ago. He would learn to twirl the ends of his moustache. He would perhaps grow fat. His head would come to be as bald as grandfather's. He would be a great man then. There were also soldiers who did not ride in cars along the road. He could hear them passing even when he did not see. Their swords rattled at their sides, and their spurs clanked. He hoped this war would last until he wore a soldier's uniform and had a sword to rattle at his side. He would cut his way right through the enemy and leave them lying bloody on the ground. He would swing his bloody sword above his head and lead the shout, "Banzai, Banzai, Banzai!" He never spoke such thoughts as these aloud to his friend Dannie. Dannie did not like to talk of war. Often on these summer evenings the neighborhood boys played a game they called "Battle". The irrigation ditch became a wide deep river. The frogs that croaked along the banks and in the black depths of the water were the enemy they had taken by surprise. With long sharp sticks they tried to spear the frogs. The one who speared the most was chosen the next day's general. Dannie said it was a cruel game. He always went back home when it began. Sometimes the other boys threw rocks at him. They always laughed at him. Tajiro never laughed or threw a stone. Dannie was his friend. He did not always understand him, but he would not hurt him. When the game was over he always went to Dannie's house and found him. The game was never mentioned. They began again where they had stopped before this game of war started. It was as if the "battle" had not been. Now, as he thought of Dannie, he remembered the paper he was to buy. Quickly he felt in his right pocket to see if the money was still there. His fingers touched the piece of paper he had wrapped it in. He was satisfied. As soon as school was out he would go quickly to the paper store. Tonight, before dark came, the plane must fly. Dannie thought it was the best plane that he had ever made. He said that it would fly farther. Well, they should see.

"The sun is hot this morning," said the boy who worked beside him.

"Yes, and I am thirsty. Shall we get a drink?" Tajiro said. They placed their rakes together on the hard ground and walked to the tall bronze monument where they had left their coats and canteens. Each filled his mouth from his own canteen and rinsed it out with vigor.

"This is the monument to the soldiers who died in the war with Russia. We read about it in our history book the other day. Do you remember? My grandfather has often brought me here. He fought in that war and in the war with China, too," Tajiro boasted.

An insistent automobile horn sounded close behind them. They stepped aside as ambulance followed ambulance slowly in a long procession, turning just beyond the shrine to rows of low new hospital buildings that filled the space up to the castle walls. Between the ambulances that passed, the boys could see the new recruits with their training officers marching, halting, turning and then marching back again across the far end of the parade ground. Tajiro said, "I suppose another hospital ship is in." When the last ambulance had passed, Tajiro and his friend turned and went back to their work in the shrine grounds. The morning's work was almost finished. Inspection over, they would march back, two by two, in complete silence to the classroom they had left. Tajiro hoped that he could stay awake this morning. Each day this seemed a harder thing to do. Sometimes, when he was reading history, the page would be just one big blur, and Sensei's voice would seem to come from somewhere far away. And every day there was a strange, hollow feeling down inside of him. He had not told his mother. He could see that she was always tired. Even when they had their evening meal together and she was ready to begin her night's work at the factory, he could see the weary drooping of her shoulders and the tired look that came into her eyes. Yesterday, when they were walking home together, he had told his grandfather about it, but his grandfather had not heard. He only rubbed Tajiro's head and said so low that he could hardly hear him, "Soon it will be time to dig the sweet potatoes."

8. The school orchestra with Mr. Palchicoffe, conductor, standing center - 1927.

CHAPTER 5
OSENTEI GARDEN

Ojii San's thoughts were on Tajiro as he hurried from Gaines Hall on his way to work. He had dug the ditch around the lilac tree, said goodbye to Mori San and then gone around the house and through the back gate to the college grounds. "Ojii San, wait!" Yuki San called. She came out to him with a piece of folded paper in her hand. "Mori San said for me to give you this. You almost got away before I saw you. I thought that you would call me for another cup of tea. Digging is not easy work when there has been no rain." Ojii San bowed his thanks. Yuki San smiled and left him. Out of sight around the dormitory, Ojii San looked inside the folded paper. A five yen bill! Far too much money for the work he had done. But he could use it. After work today he would go to the big market on the other side of town. Tajiro should have food even if it took the whole five yen to buy it. This would make the day's work easier. He slipped the money into his belt and walked on to the street as fast as his bowed legs would carry him. He seemed to be a little taller and the smile that showed his one tooth was back upon his face. Out the small side gate in the college wall and into Upper Flowing River Street. Up one block to the street's end. Then into the avenue of pines until he came to the Great Gate set in a long, white tile-capped wall. The Great Gate was closed. Stooping low, Ojii San passed within the walls through a small door at the Great Gate's side. This was where Ojii San worked. This was Osentei, the garden of the Lord Asano. When the Lord Asano died, he had bequeathed his garden to the city. It was now a public park and Ojii San was its only keeper.

Before the war a score of men had trimmed its lawns and clipped its shrubs and swept its paths each day. Since the war began, city revenues had fallen off and all the able-bodied men had gone to war. And now Ojii San did the work each day that was most needed. Visitors no longer came as they had once come, a hundred in a day. Now the Great Gate was never opened. The museum doors were closed and locked. It seemed a very lonely place with its glory gone far away. It almost seemed a sad place to Ojii San as he passed in through the gate this morning. He passed the empty gate house and took his clippers, rake and broom out of the tool house at its rear.

Tools on his shoulder, Ojii San opened the gate in the inner wall and went into the garden. The beauty of the garden in the early morning always startled him. He liked it best on a May morning when the azaleas were in bloom. Every morning when he came to work his imagination painted in the colors and the brilliance of the spring. In May, the lake reflected all the glory of the flowers around its border. The new green and red of maples traced a pattern of old brocade against the deeper green of pines. Yes, it was most beautiful in May. Yet, he loved too the scarlet of the maples in the autumn. It was hard to say which season was the best. From the shaded recesses of the low-roofed cottage by the lake, the voice of the old priest rose and fell in rhythmic cadences. Every morning all through the year it was the same. Ojii San sometimes saw the thin bent figure of the old man as he moved about within the rooms, or as he walked, head bent in contemplation, along the shady garden paths. Most often he could see him sitting at the low book-covered desk. He could hear his chanting voice whenever he was working in the garden. Since the Lord Asano died five years ago, the old priest had not left the garden. A fellow workman once told Ojii San that the Lord Asano left this house to be used by the old priest until he died. Sometimes visitors were frightened by him when they saw him on the garden paths. Ojii San knew there was nothing to be frightened of. The priest was just an old man living in a world already dead. Ojii San hoped the priest found his world more comfortable to live in than this present world.

He must get on with the work he had to do. This morning he must mend the thatched roof of the moon-gazing cottage and trim the shrubs on top of the mound at the east end of the garden. He liked to work in both these places. The moon-gazing cottage had stood unused for years. In these quick-moving times men scoffed at sentiment. They had no time for cultivating arts, no time for poetry. Ojii San felt that men were poorer. It had been different when he was a boy. On summer or autumn nights when the moon shone brightly on the Ota River, he had seen the Lord Asano and his friends gather in this very cottage to spend the best hours of the night gazing at the river and the garden in the moonlight or looking at the round disc of the moon itself. Someone would quote a poem from an old master. Other poems followed. If the poem was a long one, all would join together in reciting it. Then someone would compose a poem. Others followed. And so the night was passed. One night last September when the moon was full, Ojii San came back to the garden to see if Ota River really looked as beautiful from the moon-gazing house as he remembered it. The garden seemed more lovely than he had ever seen it. The paths he walked upon were silver, the lake a polished mirror to reflect the shadows of the trees. He walked around the lake and came close to the moon-house. Then he heard a gentle chanting. It rose and fell, then rose again and died away. He reached the moon-house. Seated on the balcony overlooking the river sat the ancient priest. The poetry he chanted to the moon was much more ancient still:

> "The sky is a sea
> Where the moon billows rise;
> And the moon is a bark;
> To the groves of the stars
> It is oaring its way."

He stopped a moment, gazing out across the river to the hills beyond. Ojii San sat down on the balcony. The old priest did not see him. Again the old man sang:

> "To what shall I compare
> This life of ours?
> It is like a boat
> Which at daybreak rows away
> And leaves no trace behind it."

Ojii San remembered one of Basho's poems that his father taught him long ago. When the old man paused Ojii San said:

> "Twas the new moon!
> Since then I have waited ----
> And lo! tonight!"

The priest turned his head and looked into the shadows. Then he looked again across the river and in full rich tones he sang:

> "Many paths there be
> To reach the mountain's height.
> But all who climb there see
> The same moon's light."

That night was one Ojii San would remember always.

He would work first on the mound and then come to the moon-house. He liked the mound. From the very top, if he looked back, he saw the castle framed in pines above the camel-back bridge that spanned the lake. If he looked ahead, he saw the river flowing just beneath him. This morning he could see three small boats, their sails filling with the first breath of a rising breeze. If he had looked a little later, they would have been out of sight behind the trees. The shrieking whistle of a locomotive tore the stillness of the garden. The heron standing at the lake's edge was startled into standing for a moment on two legs instead of one. Between the houses across the river smoke billowed and was gone. "The eight-o'clock express," Ojii San muttered, half aloud, as he stooped to pull a weed from the path's edge.

CHAPTER 6
SHOPPING AT HONDORI

Mori San opened the small door in the red brick wall and held it while Kihara San and Hata San passed through. Then she stepped into the street, closing the door softly after her. "It is already after seven," said Hata San. All the way to Kihara San's they walked close to the walls that lined the street to keep within the shade. Mori San said, "In America the streets are twice as broad as this. There are no walls around the houses and big trees shade the streets. The people walk on sidewalks----" She paused and looked around her. "I wish I could remember not to talk about such things," she said.

Hata San, too, scanned the street. "It seems quite safe this morning," she said quietly. "Perhaps it is too early for your friend from the police."

"Oh, he will be along," Mori San replied as softly as she could. "He hasn't missed a single time since 1942. We have grown to be quite friendly. When he comes for his monthly visit now I always ask him in, and we drink tea. He eyes me with suspicion for the first 10 minutes of the interview. He scowls and makes his voice sound quite ferocious. Then he slips his book into his pocket and relaxes as he drinks tea. He shows me pictures of his baby, and we talk of many things. Then suddenly he remembers and grows stiff and cold again." At Kihara San's big gate they paused long enough for the usual farewells. They turned into the sun now, and Kihara San stood watching until the two parasols bobbed out of sight around the next turn in the street.

"Tadaima -- I am here now," called Kihara San as she closed the sliding door. As if by magic, Tamako San appeared from behind the lacquered spirit screen that seemed to fill the entrance way.

From her knees she bowed her welcome. "It is good that you have come," she said. Rising, she followed her mistress into the house.

"Has Kihara come in yet?" her mistress asked.

"He is not here," the servant answered as quietly as the question had been asked.

Kihara San had not seen her husband since the night before. He came in a little before dinner time. Long before he came she made sure the bath was ready and laid out his clean clothes. The entrance bell sounded and she heard his steps along the hall. He threw his hat upon the table. "Has the paper come?" he asked. He stripped, standing there before her, and went into the bath. His discarded clothes lay on the floor in little heaps.

She picked them up and carried them into the kitchen. Handing them to a maid, she said, "Will you hang the master's clothes somewhere to dry?" She waited for him in the dining room and sat down after him. He sat across the table from her drinking heated <u>sake</u>, cup after cup of the light amber wine. She told the maid to set the food before him, but no sign did he make that it was there.

His face grew flushed with the warm wine. Then pushing his cup from him, he rose. "I must go out again," he said.

"But must you go before you eat?" Kihara San replied.

"I do not want the food," he answered.

She heard the entrance bell again as the door closed after him. All night she and the maids were alone in the great house. They went out together when the air-raid sirens sounded and came back again together to the dark and silent house. And now, "He is not here," Tamako San was saying. They went into the living room.

"If you have nothing special here for me to do this morning," Tamako San continued, "I think that I shall do some shopping on Hondori. The mosquito nets need patching very badly. Perhaps at one of the big cloth stores I can find something we can use to cover up the holes. Someone was saying at the bath last night that a shop down on Hondori had some soap for sale yesterday. I suppose there will be nothing left today, but it may be worth looking into. I shall go now so that I can be there when the shops open. I shall be back in time to get lunch ready."

Kihara San said, "While you are there, see what you can find to send to Sa-chan. He will be expecting something soon. I am at my wit's end. It seems that we have sent him everything."

In a few moments Tamako San was back again, ready for the street. "There is nothing I can do for you before I go?" she asked.

"Nothing. Go, and hurry back," her mistress answered. "I shall write to Sa-chan while you are away. If you find the cloth to patch the nets, we can work on them together this afternoon." How lucky she was to have Tamako San through these hard years, she thought, as she watched her turn and leave the room.

No one would have thought Tamako San a servant. As she hurried from the house this morning she had the air of any housewife on an early morning mission. Her thoughts were with her mistress as she turned into the street. She was glad now that she had come to work for the Kiharas. Five years ago she hesitated long before deciding to come. For more than 20 years she had been in service with the foreign ladies at the school. All she knew of cooking and of keeping house she learned from them. She was afraid she knew the wrong things to go to work at her age in the house of a rich Japanese. But the foreign ladies had closed their houses and gone away. She had gone all the way to Kobe with her last foreign mistress. She watched the big ship sail away into the mist. Part of the mist filled her eyes. The foreign teachers had been kind to her. She would never find another place that paid so well. Perhaps she would stop working, she said that day. She felt old and deserted.

She came back to Hiroshima because she knew no other home. Kihara San had said, "Come live with me." And she had gone. Now she was glad. Kihara San was another lonely soul. Tamako San cooked, cleaned and sewed for her. But most of all she was there for Kihara San to talk to on the long nights while she sat waiting for the master of the house to return. They always talked of other things. No word ever passed between them about the man they waited for. This morning, nothing had been said about him. On these nights, after waiting through long hours together, at the first sound of his wooden clogs on the flagstones at the gate, Tamako San would bow goodnight and go to her own room at the far end of the house.

These men! she thought, as she stepped aside to keep from being knocked down by a bicycle. A woman was never happy until she had a son. She brought him into the world, and from the first moment of his life she lavished every care upon him. From his first conscious moment he was lord of whatever world was his. He grew into boyhood thinking that no wish of his should be denied. His wish was paramount, his will the law. When he came to manhood and his world had grown, he still held himself to be the center of whatever world was his. When he was little and was naughty, he was laughed at and called cute. When he had grown too old to be called cute, he still was laughed at for his greater naughtiness. She knew. She had helped to spoil three brothers. If she had a son, she would have given him his way. It was the way of woman even though it brought her sorrow in the end.

It must have been the thought of the son she might have had that loosed the flood of memories in her mind. That door she usually kept closed. Her feet moved now along the familiar streets with no guidance on her part. She was back in a little country village, and she was just 16. It was her wedding day. The wedding feast was over. She had tasted nothing. The man she had married sat across the room from her. She wondered what he looked like. She had not raised her eyes to look at him or to look at anything since the ceremonies began. Her neck was weary with the weight of the heavy combs that held her hair. She wondered what the house was like, this house that was her home. Soon the wedding guests would say goodnight, and leave her here in this new world. She still could feel the chill that crossed her heart. Wine was flowing freely. The men's speech had thickened, and they began to sing ribald songs. They clapped their hands and shouted in the pauses between words. Her husband's mother and his sister led her from the room to the bridal chamber. Here stood the bridal chests and boxes she had brought with her from her home. A wave of homesickness swept over her. On the floor were spread the silk pallets she had brought, hers and her husband's, side by side. Her wedding garments were removed. She was prepared for bed. She lay down and pulled the covers close as she waited for this husband whose face she had not seen. She had no words for the sick horror of that night with a husband by her side who was a man unknown, half-drunk and twice her age.

In the morning he roused her early. "Come," he said. "You must work beside me in the fields today." For three days she worked, and then she left him. She had not known what working in the fields could mean. She had not stopped to think of consequences. She just ran away. The days that followed were vague shadows in her memory. The walk....Those 15 miles back to her own village....Her shame before her mother....Her father's anger. She would have been frightened but for the greater horror she had fled. Her father said, since she had chosen, she could make her own way in the world....The clanging of the street-car bell awoke her to the present. She stepped back quickly as the rocking car swept by.

She looked around her. The streets were filled with people on their way to work. She crossed the street-car tracks, pushed her way through the crowds that stood waiting for the cars and hurried on her way. In front of Fukuya, the big department store, a line stood waiting for the doors to open. "I shall come here last, when I have finished with my other shopping," Tamako San said to herself. She stopped a little farther down the street at the fruit store where she always traded. A woman with a baby on her back was removing the last wooden panel of the door. She placed it neatly with the others against the inside wall.

"Gomen-nasai, excuse me, please!" Tamako San called as she entered.

"O-haiyo gozaimasu, good morning!" the woman turned to greet her. "It has been a long time since we have seen you. I am sorry we have nothing more to offer you this morning, only a few figs and these poor loquats. These melons grow here in Hiroshima. They are just beginning to come in, and the price is very high. I am expecting some nice grapes later in the morning. I could send some later in the day, perhaps."

Tamako San picked up a melon. "How much is this one?" she asked the woman. "Please weigh it for me, and I shall take some loquats, too. If you will wrap them for me I shall stop and get them on my way back home. How is your husband's father?"

"He never leaves his bed," replied the woman. "It makes it very hard to keep the store and care for him. Now that my husband and his brother have both gone to war, I have no one to help me."

"I hope the war will soon be over so that we can live a normal life again. If the grapes come in put some of them away for me. Kihara San is very fond of them."

"I thank you very much," the woman said.

Tamako San went out into the street. The fruit store made her sad. It had been the richest, finest fruit store in the city. Its stands had never been so empty. She remembered them piled high. Oranges from islands in the Inland Sea; pineapples, lemons, bananas, pomelos from Formosa; apples, pears and melons from Korea and Hokkaido; persimmons, grapes and peaches. Now only loquats, figs and melons grown in Hiroshima. No longer any fruit from far romantic places.

Tamako San walked on. A few steps more and she would turn into Hondori where there were more fine shops than on any other street in all the city. If only she could fly instead of weaving in and out through all this traffic, she thought, as she turned into the street. Waves of sound, diverse yet intermingled, descended full upon her ears. The gritting of metal cart wheels upon the pavement; the short ringing sound of the iron shoes on horses hoofs; the click-clack, click-clack of the wooden geta men and women wore; the flip of feather dusters where stores were being put in order for the day; bicycle bells, a million of them with as many different tones; the tinkle of the entrance bells as shop doors were opened; the deeper tones of the bells rung by the "sandwich-men" and the slow, desperate, hollow sound of the rhythm of their steps; the lonesome bell of a lone jinrikisha and the muffled pad-pad of the runner's soft-soled shoes; and in the distance, the shrill whistle of the fish-man, the clang of street cars and the slow tolling of a temple bell. Tamako San's thoughts were as mixed and as varied as the sounds she heard. How hungry and discouraged that old brown horse looks. Amazing how he pulls that heavy cart. How worn and tired the geta look as they move up and down and forward on the pavement. Mine must be just as worn. On the bicycles, so many women. They always look a little strange. Better though in mompei-pants than in kimono. Most of the shops are already open. Everybody gets up early now, except those people who do their working in the night time and their sleeping in the day. That geisha who just passed in the jinrikisha has been up all night, no doubt. I wonder how she feels in all that finery when she sees other women in their shabby clothes. Perhaps she never sees. What is it that the sandwich-men are advertising? -"This afternoon from two, tonight from seven, see the latest war news at the News Theatre near the Falcon Bridge. Filmed by the Asahi Newspaper." - I am tired of seeing news reels. They show us nothing else these days. I wonder if that fish-man really has some fish to sell. The temple bell reminds me of the summers when I used to go to Nikko with the foreign teachers from the school. It sounds so peaceful and so far away.

Sounds, colors. Waves of color met her eyes; waves that broke, receded, and then broke again upon her consciousness. Blues, reds, golds, greens, yellows, mauves and pinks from geta on display in shoe store windows; from fans in the window of the fan store down the street, fans made of paper over split bamboo or of silk over slender sticks of sandalwood; from kimono on the figures in the cloth store windows, from bolts of cloth unrolled in gay profusion and from obi draped to show their brightest hues; from jewels, rubies, sapphires, emeralds and rich old jade in jewelers' windows; from china shops with shelves of old Imari and Kutani around the walls and a wealth of new and cheaper wares piled high on top and underneath the long low tables for display. The colors in the street itself were not so gay. The dirty khaki of soldier and civilian uniforms; faded coolie blue; the deep blues and blacks of women's clothing; the washed out grays of factory workers' uniforms; unpainted wagons, unpainted shop fronts; the old wood of gutter covers. The only brightness outside of shop windows came from the glint of sunlight on the white uniform of a nurse who hurried on her way to work and on the whiter uniform of a policeman standing in the doorway of the police station farther down the street. Tamako San was thinking, those fans in that window, the ones with poems written on them, how elegant they are! And those smaller fans with cherry blossoms on them. I believe I like those big fans that the men use best. Just looking at that fan with the fat Buddha on it makes me want to laugh. I wonder if they sell fans now-a-days or if they keep them in the windows just for show. Of course nobody buys that bright kimono cloth. I wonder why they put it out. Maybe brides still buy it. Those stones look odd without gold settings. That new silver looking metal makes the stones look cheap and artificial. I suppose nobody buys them. The tax would be too high. I'm glad they keep them in the window anyway. It makes a spot of color that I like. I must stop here at this china store as I come back down the street. I might find a salad dish to match the one I broke the other day. How worn and shabby everything here in the street looks! Like the geta all of us are wearing, even that nurse just ahead of me. I wonder which hospital she belongs to. Probably the one just around the corner. She walks so fast she must be late.... Just as Tamako San passed the police station, the policeman standing in the doorway turned his watch face to the light to see the time. The sun shone full upon his arm. For an instant, the quick flash of light reflected from the crystal struck Tamako San directly in the eyes, blotting out the color and the drabness of the windows and the street. The arm fell. The light was gone. Tamako San looked past the white of the policeman to the clock upon the wall inside. It was almost eight o'clock. She must hurry, there was shopping to be done.

After Tamako San left the house to do her shopping on Hondori, Kihara San sat down at the low desk and took a roll of writing paper from the drawer. Wetting her brush-pen in the black ink, she began a letter to her son. She wrote: "Your father is away from home for several days on business..."

CHAPTER 7
WILLOW GARDENS

At the lower end of Flowing River Street a narrow side street led off to the left. Two shops that faced Flowing River Street flanked the narrow street on either side, windowless and gray. Behind the shops, the narrow street spread itself into a broad open square around three sides of which stood big, hotel-like houses of new, unpainted wood. The houses were ornately carved around doors, along high-railed balconies and under wide-spread eaves. In a dozen shops on Flowing River Street a dozen clocks told different times of day. One said seven-thirty, one ten minutes after eight, others took a middle ground between the two. Suddenly a radio blared forth from somewhere on the street. With calm disregard for all the clocks a brisk voice said, "All set for the eight o'clock morning exercises. Ready. Go."

Then to the strains of "Shall We Gather At The River" came the shouted "<u>ichi</u>, ni, san, shi, <u>go</u>, roku, shichi, hachi -- <u>one</u>, two, three, four, <u>five</u>, six, seven, eight." Standing in his doorway next to the narrow street, a shop keeper extended his arm to the side eight times, then forward; bent his body back eight times, then forward; stooped, squatted, twisted, turned; up, down, up, down; hands over and around, all in time to the music and the counting. In front of him, the street was as alive as Tamako San had found Hondori. Cars hurried in and out of a taxi stand. Bicycles, bent on urgent missions, careened madly between carts and hurrying pedestrians. A line some two blocks long moved slowly toward a grain store down the street where the weekly rationing of rice was being sold. In front of the flower shop at the corner of the narrow street an old woman unloaded zinnias, gladiolas, marigolds and roses from a half-empty cart. All this on Flowing River Street.

In the narrow street and on the court beyond no sign of life was visible. The bamboo window curtains of the houses were rolled down. A bob-tailed, yellow cat appeared lazily from the open door of one of the houses, crossed the court and disappeared from view. Life in these houses stopped when morning came. At night they were alive with music, song and drunken laughter, but now they were houses of the dead; for these were Machiai, or Geisha Houses, that only came alive in the late hours of the afternoon. Here was a village living a life apart from the city that surrounded it. It was a village owned and operated by shrewd businessmen. Its inhabitants were some 200 women listed by their owners under Assets - Goods and Chattels. Despite the years of war, this business went on much as always. When other businesses were failing or just managing to hang on, here in the village profits soared. Men's desire rose with the rising tide of war. Of course much of the profit went back into the business because upkeep was expensive. There were always new girls to be bought. They were more difficult to find and more expensive these days when jobs for women could be found with ease and for good pay. But there were still men who were willing to sell their daughters for a few hundred yen with which to feed themselves or pay their debts. Younger girls came cheaper and were easier to train. The years of training must be long in any case. It was not easy to produce a geisha skillful in the arts of singing and of dancing and in the ways of pleasing men.

On this morning, in the largest of these houses just off Flowing River Street, a man sat working at a low desk near the open entranceway. In even rows on two walls of the foyer were displayed pictures of the women of the house. They were placed here to assist the patron in his choice. From time to time the man behind the desk would scan the pictures, write something down, place a sheaf of papers in a file and take more papers out. He was a very busy man, for he was manager of this largest

Machiai, Yanagi Koen or the Willow Gardens. His name was Nishida.

As he lifted a fresh sheaf of papers from the file Nishida looked up at the clock. He sighed. Seven-thirty. "I have sat here for two hours," he muttered to himself. From a little bamboo basket by his side he took a damp towel and wiped the perspiration from his face.

"How can it be so damned hot this early in the morning," he said aloud. "Oi, oi, bring me some fresh tea," he called impatiently.

A woman's head appeared between the panels of the sliding door. "You shall have your tea," she said, "But do not yell so. You will wake the entire house. In all this house with all these people it is you and I alone who do not sleep. The more they rest at seven-thirty the more money will they earn for us tonight. I think their sleeping is of more importance than your tea. But I shall bring it to you."

"What a pig of a wife," scowled Nishida. "But she is right. I should not be impatient when my pile of gold grows higher with each day." And he bent again above his work. He must check the bills this morning and draw some money from the bank. The collectors would be calling on him before the morning ended. But first he must check his order sheets. He thumbed the sheets of paper on the desk before him. "Tonight should be a record night," he thought. An army captain wanted 15 girls for a banquet he was giving at the Besso on the other side of town. It must be a big party. Perhaps the captain hoped for a promotion and was putting all his money into this one fling. Well, he would see that girls from Willow Gardens did not come for nothing. The honorable banker wanted three for a private dinner, did he? And he wanted Tazuko? That little Tazuko was being asked for by more people every day. When he had bought her she was such a tiny thing he had been afraid that she would turn out badly. He had just been letting her go out these last two months. Already she had brought in more business than some of those who had been with him for twice the time. He must call her in and talk to her. She must have something he had failed to see. Here were two requests for her tonight. He would give her to the banker, but he would charge him for her too. Bankers, though, seemed made of money, like Kihara who came here every night. "He is a fool," he thought, "but he brings in good money. That Hana works them all. She is making herself a soft bed to retire on," and he chuckled to himself.

His wife brought in the tea. She sat down on the mat covered floor beside him. She poured hot tea in his cup and watched him while he sipped it noisily. "We will need all of the jinrikishas for tonight," he said to her. "When you go out to do your morning buying will you check the taxi stand? We will need at least five cars tonight. They will not have that many, but if they will let us use as many as they have.... I am going to the bank this morning." He looked around carefully, then opened a small drawer. Stealthily he lifted out a dirty canvas bag and gave it to his wife. "Put this away where you have put the other. There is no use in letting taxes eat up all our profits. What we do not put down upon the books the government will never know about. They will see my bank account. That is enough. Go and hide the money quickly before the house begins to stir." Again he turned a sheet of paper on the desk before him. The yellow house cat brushed his knee in passing. The sliding door creaked gently as his wife opened it, passed through and closed it after her.

Upstairs in this same house Saburo Kihara lay asleep on silken pallets on the clean, white, mat covered floor. While his wife, Kihara San, sat at home writing her morning letter to their son, Kihara stirred and stirred again. He turned heavily onto his back. His bleary, swollen eyes half opened. He shook his head, closed his eyes, then opened them again. "Where in the name of all the Buddhist devils am I?" he asked aloud. He sat up cross-legged on his bed. A thousand red-hot needles pierced his head and ran in zigzags down his spine. He lay down and closed his eyes again. A moment more and he remembered.

Last night he had gone home for dinner. He meant to stay. He told himself that he would think no more of Hana. The last time he had seen her at the Willow Gardens she made demands upon him that were far beyond his power to meet. She was a hard and grasping woman. But she was beautiful. For two years she had been a fever in his blood.... Again the burning needles through his head!.... He remembered well the first time he saw her. He had been invited to a dinner at the Fuji Koen, the most talked of restaurant in town. It was an evening in early summer just two years ago. The host was lavish in his entertainment. There must have been 100 geishas. Before they sat down at the tables in the long banquet hall, the guests had walked about the park, with geisha escort, to watch carp swimming in the lake, to see monkeys in their cages in the zoo, and to climb the little artificial hillside where the fountains had their source. While standing at the peak of this small hill he saw her with a group below him. She was laughing as she stepped from stone to stone across the stream that ran down to the lake. The wine and blue of her kimono made a perfect setting for her skin. In one hand she held her lacquered geta and her tabi. With her other hand she held her bright kimono high above her knees as she stuck first one foot then the other into the clear running stream. She was still there playing in the water when he and his companions came down from the mound. They were looking at the waterfall that made a misty veil across the rocks set in the hillside. Suddenly colored lights flooded all the garden, turning the spray of the little waterfall into a rainbow background for the girl standing deep in the water. In that moment he knew he wanted her. He had not known then how hard and grasping she could be. That night he learned her name and the name of the house she came from. Hana Chan they called her, Little Flower, and she came from Willow Gardens in the court off Flowing River Street.

Again Kihara turned upon his bed. The piercing needles stopped his thinking for a moment. Again his mind cleared. Sitting last night at his own table he had seen her face in every cup of sake he drank. She had been with every moment of the long hot day. The night before they spent hours quarreling because she wanted gifts, gifts, always gifts. For every hour of pleasure that she gave him he paid dearly and far beyond his means. And now she wanted a diamond ring. Her friend, Haru Chan, had just received one. It was the most beautiful that she had ever seen. She must find someone rich enough to give her one. All day at work the thought of her tormented him. He could not buy a diamond ring. His wife had put her money into war bonds, all that was left each year when taxes had been paid. Hana had already cost him more than his allowance for the two years he had known her. It was sometime yesterday afternoon that the thought had come to him. His wife kept all her jewels in a safe deposit box at the bank. He had the key. She had not opened it for five years now. There were diamonds there. She would not ever wear them all. She might not even miss one if he took it. He chose one of the most beautiful and slipped it into his pocket, just in case he wished to use it. All the time he was bathing he told himself, "I will stay at home tonight. I will not let that woman ruin me. There is no reason to her constant nagging. I shall read my paper after dinner and then go to bed."

The sake he drank stirred his blood. He could not face his wife across the table. He felt she knew that after his bath he had wrapped the ring in paper and put it in the purse that slightly protruded from the folds of his kimono. It was then that he left the table. "Must you go without your dinner?" she had asked.

He went straight to the Willow Gardens. Hana kept him waiting for awhile. Then she came to him still pouting. She knew that pouting made her all the more delightful. He said, "I hope that you are ready. We are going out to dinner. Tonight we celebrate."

"And what is there to celebrate?" she asked.

"This," he answered as he handed her the ring. She slipped it on her finger, and a light broke in her eyes. Her lips smiled again. Then she was in his arms, and the anguish of the day melted....

A ray of sunlight found its way through the bamboo curtains straight into Kihara's eyes. Startled, he raised himself upon his elbow and looked around him. This was a room in Willow Gardens. He still did not know how he came to be here. Last night, in this room, he had given the ring to Hana. She had flung herself into his arms, and time had stopped. How much later it had been he did not know, but suddenly they both were very hungry. While Hana dressed he sent a maid to call a taxi. They went to Fuji Koen and ate supper in a small room overlooking a small, cool garden. Hana had continued to be kind. He could not remember what they had eaten, but he did know there had been more <u>sake</u>. And that was all that he remembered. Now here he was again in this same room. It must be morning. That was a ray of sunlight that roused him just now. "Hana! Hana!" he called loudly. She was nowhere in the room. No answer. Then he shouted, "Oi! Oi!" and clapped his hands loudly as he called. In a moment the sliding door was opened, and a sleepy-eyed, old woman, bowing, asked, "Danna Sama, did you call?"

"Where is Hana?" Kihara asked her, "and why am I still here at this absurd hour of the morning?"

"Hana San is sleeping, my most worthy master. She was very weary when she finally brought you in a few short hours ago. I myself helped put you in this bed. We thought it best for you to spend the night here. If you wish to rise now I shall help you with your bath. I think that Hana San should be allowed her sleep and so do you I am quite sure." She came into the room. "It is early yet. Why do you not sleep again? I shall call you when you say. Rest a little longer, and then a good hot bath and breakfast will make you equal to the day." Kihara remembered that he had his watch on. He looked to see what time it was. Eight-ten. He could sleep another hour and reach the bank by ten. Gratefully, he sank back on his pallet and closed his eyes against the light. The servant watched him for a moment and left the room, closing the door softly behind her.

CHAPTER 8
SERA SENSEI'S MEMORIES

I n the quiet of the big house Kihara San wrote on. A mound of soft, white paper streaked with black lay fold on fold beside the desk. From across the garden wall came the distant hum of morning in the city. From the oleanders in the garden the cicadas complained unceasingly. Atop the lacquered Chinese chest in the corner of the room the French clock ticked away the passing minutes. A quiet rustle marked each fold added to the growing mound of paper by the desk.

"Early this morning," Kihara San wrote, "I walked over to see Mori San for a few minutes. She and Hata San walked back with me to the front gate on their way to Hijiyama. Yesterday afternoon on my way home from the hospital, I stopped by the high school dormitory to see Sera Sensei. She sends her best regards to you...."

Sera Sensei slowly turned the pages of the album she and Kihara San had looked through together yesterday. She would look at it once more before she put it back upon the shelf. Breakfast was so early on these summer mornings that by seven-thirty the morning seemed half gone. Already she had seen her 50 charges off to classes and made her morning round of room inspection. By eight o'clock the cook should be in for Monday planning. This hour, however, was her own. Somehow, through this last year, she had come to need more hours like this, hours that were her own. She tired so much more quickly than ever before. Perhaps the tiredness this morning came from the album lying open upon the table. It made her very conscious of the years that lay behind her....

The stone steps leading to the temple on the hillside looked much whiter in the picture than they really were. The wall, though, had always seemed to grow out of the trees. Strange how much more there was to see in the picture of a place you knew than in a picture of a place you had never seen. To her this picture was much more than white stone steps leading to a gate in a wall half hidden by trees, behind which sloping temple roofs nestled against still other trees. To her the wall was red, and the trees that partly covered it were a deep, dark green. In the picture the panels of the gate were closed, and its low-hanging roof of tiles hid the carving above the panels. To her the dull, red panel doors stood always open. Above the panels, close beneath the gray tiled roof, her eyes could see carved lotus blossoms floating on blue painted water. The big pink blossom at the left had been her special flower. She had chosen it because it seemed so real. Many times as she stood beneath it she had been sure she caught a subtle fragrance. Inside the gate stood the house where she was born. The wall hid it in the picture. But it was there, close beside the temple, just below the curving roof on the right. A polished, sloping gallery joined it to the temple. What fun sliding on it in her stocking feet had been! One of the first things she could remember was climbing from the gallery to her nurse's back and being carried through the gate, down the long stone steps to walk beneath the cherry trees that bloomed along the road below.

The cherry blossoms always made her think about her mother. She was delicate and fragile like the cherry flowers. There was no picture of her in the album. All her life she refused to have one taken. Sera Sensei did not need a picture though to see her. She could see her sitting in the room just off the gallery. A flood of winter sunshine filled the room and lit up the colors in the cloth she sewed. She could see her on a bright November day sweeping up dry leaves from around the temple. She could see her on a rainy winter afternoon writing letters on thin rice paper. Those long rainy winter afternoons! They had been hard when she was still a little girl. There was so little she could do. She would play at keeping house awhile, slide down the gallery until her legs ached, and then begin to beg her mother, "Oka San, let me see your wedding dress, the black one with the trees and flowers and birds embroidered on it." Then from the top drawer in the big camphor chest that had been a part of her mother's dowry the kimono would be lifted to the floor and carefully unfolded. She could close her eyes now and feel the softness of the silk and the roughness of the raised embroidery. She loved to run her fingers over the rough trunk of the old plum tree and stroke the softness of the white blossoms on its branches. She had sold her own wedding outfit, but this kimono that had been her mother's still lay folded in its white paper cover on the top shelf of the camphor chest. There it was across the room.

On such an afternoon, when the wedding dress was lying out upon the floor, she had her first lesson in embroidery. Many more had followed. There had been lessons, too, in sewing and cooking, and hours and hours of flower arrangement and tea ceremony. Here was a picture of her taken when she was eleven. It was New Year's Day. She was wearing the new dress kimono that was her mother's New Year gift. The pine branches in the bamboo vase beside her she had arranged that very morning by herself. As soon as she finished her bean soup with rice cakes, she had gone into the yard to cut the branches. Arranging them had been her first act of the new year because her wish for this year was to grow adept at flower arrangement. Her mother had admired her work and said that it was done quite well, so she had her picture taken with the vase of pine beside her.

The somber priest in Buddhist robes, looking up a moment from the open books on the table before him, was her father. He had never quite forgiven her for being born a girl. The temple had been handed down from father to an eldest son for five long generations. And now his only child was not a son. But for him the Buddhist doctrines he taught were laws to live by, so he set himself to learn more of the doctrines of acceptance and resignation. Through the years he adjusted himself more and more to life as he found it. With her he had been stern, but always kind. He was her first and greatest teacher. One day when she was five he called her to him. "You are old enough to learn to read," he said. "Tomorrow morning when the temple services are over you may come into my study. I shall be waiting for you there. At first I think that we will study only on the odd days of the months. The odd days are the lucky ones." For 10 years he had been her teacher. Much that he tried to teach she could not understand, but there was much that became a part of her. He taught her how to read and how to write. He was patient with her while she learned to hold her writing brush, and showed her how to make the up-strokes and the down-strokes. He taught her how to add and subtract, then how to divide and multiply on his own abacus. When she had learned to move the rings swiftly and correctly, he gave her an ivory abacus of her own. It was in a lacquered box, wrapped in a square of bright red silk. The ivory had grown yellow with the years, but she still used it to make her monthly statement for the office or to check the cook's accounts.

Above all other things, she cherished the Zen-Buddhist doctrines he had taught her. Life was a thing that lasted but for a moment. Man's body was a house built in a wilderness. He must learn to overcome the evils and the dangers that beset him. This he could do only through the mastery of spirit over matter. He must find the Middle Path and walk in it. This path brought vision to his eyes, understanding to his heart. To walk in it was to find the road to peace and to a higher wisdom. It meant the loss of sensual desire, ill-will toward others, and one's own ignorance and stupidity. It led to self-control and made man kind to all men everywhere. He had taught her the art of quiet meditation and of calmness under stress. He had taught her where and how to look for beauty and how to treasure it. The eyes in the picture looked straight into hers. For a moment she was a small girl again sitting opposite the man at the table. With hands folded in her lap she bowed to him in humble thanks for all that he had given her.

She turned a page and then another. The tea-house! How her father had enjoyed the building of it. She had helped him choose the site for it, across the temple garden close to the old red wall. In those months while the house was slowly growing she had learned the meaning of each simple detail of construction. She could not remember just when this picture had been made, but it was taken long after the house was finished because the trees had grown around it so that the house was almost hidden. The thatched roof stood out clearly against the tall pines in the rear. Only a corner of the low entrance door was visible, and the stone basin which held the clear cool water for the purification of guests who came for tea was almost hidden by the tea-olive and nandina bushes they had planted by its side. How cool and quiet it all looked! Her father had interpreted for her the complicated symbolism of Ceremonial Tea. He had said, "The art of tea drinking, or Cha-no-yu, is a religion of the art of life. The stepping stones that lead across the pond to the tea-house form the path of self-illumination man must walk upon before he understands the art of living. That is why one never speaks when walking to the tea-house. He must walk this path alone. Only through silent meditation can one come to know himself. Through self-illumination one goes on to self-control. All this you learn through the tea ceremony." Self-control, politeness, delicacy, --- three essentials to the art of living --- all of them she had learned from the art of drinking tea. How pleasant it would be on this uncomfortable August morning to walk again along that garden path into the coolness and aloofness of that tea-house. Perhaps, there in the quiet contemplation of the simple beauty all around her she could lose this growing sense of impending danger hanging over and around her. It had been with her now for days. Perhaps this constant thinking back into the past was bad for one. But what better could one find to think about? Surely not the present with its horror and uncertainty. Nor the future, at her age, when every day seemed improbable of a tomorrow.... She looked at the clock. It was almost eight. A

few more minutes and the present would be forced upon her....
She turned another page.

A piece of thin, white rice paper fluttered to the floor.
She had forgotten this was in the album. It was a watercolor
painting of a morning-glory. Her father had painted it one
August morning many, many years ago. Every year he grew
morning-glories. That year they had been particularly beautiful.
Ten of them, each in its own separate flower pot, stood on a
stone near the pool's edge. Every day he watered them and
trained the vines around the bamboo trellises. When August
came the first flowers bloomed. That summer he had waited long
for one particular plant to bloom. Then one morning a bud that
had been growing larger day by day opened wide before the rising
sun. It was a blossom different from any other morning-glory
they had ever seen. It was so delicate it seemed a breath of air
would tear it from its stem. Her father looked at it for a long
time and then turned and went into the house without a word.
When he came back, in his hands were a drawing board with
paper pinned upon it and his painting box. She had not known
until then that he could paint. This was the picture he had
painted. Somehow he had caught all the delicacy of color and
frailty of the flower. Beneath the morning-glory he had written:

> "Asagao ni
> Tsurube torarete,
> Morai-mizu!"

"Keep this picture and learn this poem of the Lady
Chiyo," he said. "You are too young to read the poem now, but
it tells of the Lady Chiyo who went to the well one morning to
draw water, and found a morning-glory vine twined round the
bucket. Rather than tear the vine away and waste the beauty of
its flowers, she went to her neighbor's well and borrowed water
for the day. When you find a thing of beauty it is worth making
sacrifices for, even though you know that it will last no longer
than today."

This morning she had awakened early. The morning-glories on the trellis just outside her door were full of blossoms. She remembered Chiyo's poem and her father's words. Now the blossoms were all closed against the burning summer heat. Their beauty had lasted but a moment. Perhaps real beauty lived on only in the heart. She was glad that all the beauty her father had created for her was not contained in this one thin sheet of rice paper. A poem he taught her from the Kokinshu came to her:

> "I know that my life
> Has no assurance of tomorrow;
> But today,
> So long as darkness has not fallen,
> I will grieve for him who has passed away."

She turned the pages of the album quickly now. It seemed that all the people who had made her life had died before her. When one grows old, so few are left.... Here she was pictured with some classmates at Gaines Sensei's school. It still seemed strange sometimes that she had found her way here. How carefully her father planned her life, but not one thing he planned had come about! She should take a "yoshi" for a husband, a priest to run her father's temple. She would have a son, of course, to carry on where his father should leave off. But her father died. Her mother thought it best for her to go to school and Gaines Sensei's school was nearest. After two years she wanted to become a Christian! Her mother had not understood at first, but she had made her see. They sold the temple. It was still there among the green trees on the hillside. Not long ago she climbed the worn steps to stand with bowed head beside the two graves inside the dull red gate....

The middle of her life had passed as quickly as the leaves she was turning. Graduation. Marriage. Her little son. That day when there was neither son nor husband. Cold fear, then, and desperation. Gaines Sensei's invitation to come back to the school to teach. Acceptance and deep gratitude. How proud she was of that first picture with the faculty. If she had kept a picture for each year, this year there would be fifty. Looking at them now she wondered why she kept so many. Some meant nothing to her now. No doubt it was as well that one forgot. She rose and crossed the room to put the album in its place upon the shelf. She heard the cook's step in the hallway. She took the ivory abacus from its red silk wrapping and turned to face the problems of the day.

CHAPTER 9
HIROSHIMA
JOGAKUIN STUDENTS

A t school the morning hours moved in a regular routine. Already one class hour was finished and a second had begun. In the high school buildings a thousand bobbed black heads were bent above various problems of the moment. Some were reading history aloud in high stilted voices. Some were sewing, seated at low tables on the floor. Others worked at mathematics problems or listened to the Ethics teacher's exposition of the latest rescript of the Emperor. In the old gymnasium one class played touch ball; another worked among flowers in the garden just outside. From somewhere came the sound of singing classes, and the science lecture room was full.

The second year class was sewing. They were learning to make the sleeves of a kimono, and Masako San was troubled. This was her first year of sewing. She liked it even less than she had thought she would. As she thrust the needle in and out and pulled the long thread after it she said to herself, "If I only had some soft bright cloth to sew on it would help my feelings some. This old cloth will scarcely hold the thread when I have made the seam. I do not like drab, faded things." She looked around her. Everybody else's cloth was faded too. Perhaps if she tried thinking about something pleasant the hour would pass more quickly, and the next class hour would come. Next hour was singing. She liked her singing class the best of all. Sensei had promised they could sing "Nemure, Sleep, baby sleep," her favorite song. When she sang it she felt as if she held her baby sister in her arms. How she would like to see that baby sister! It had been months since she was home. The baby would be three years old before she saw her -- if she ever did get home. Now with all the bombings they might not ever let her go. Kure had been bombed and so had Fukuyama. When she went home she changed trains in Fukuyama. Her mother wrote for her to stay on in Hiroshima. It seemed much safer there.

Last night when they had come back from the air-raid shelter she and Shizuko San, her roommate, had talked for a long, long time. Shizuko San lived in Okayama, almost as big a city as Hiroshima. There were shops and picture shows that she could go to every day. But Masako lived up in the mountains and had never seen a city until last year when she came to school here in Hiroshima. Last night Masako talked about her home so much that when she went to sleep she dreamed about it. She was five years old again. She and her younger brother were playing house under the big acacia tree. "You must cook the rice," he said, "while I go out and gather wood."

"Yes, I will draw the water from the well and fix your food," she said. She stopped beside the well to bow three times before the water god enshrined there. The water god had spoken. "You are going far away beyond the mountains," he said. She went into the kitchen for a bamboo sieve. She must wash the rocks she used for rice before she put them on to cook. From the god shelf in the kitchen she heard a little sigh. The kitchen god was peeping at her from behind the bright red curtain of his shining little house. He jumped onto the table and down onto the floor. "Watch me dance," he told her as he hopped about the kitchen on one leg. "Hata-po-po, hata-po-po," he sang in a high squeaky voice. Suddenly he stopped and gave a long shrill whistle. From the other rooms and from outside all kinds of little gods came trooping in. "Don't be afraid," they said. "We will not hurt you. We like this house. Everybody in it is as happy as can be. We like to live with happy people." And then they all took hands and danced together. The noise they made grew louder and still louder. She covered up her ears and screamed as loud as she could scream.... She opened her eyes and Shizuko San was shaking her. It was morning in Hiroshima and time to go to school.

"Hurry," said her roommate, "or we shall miss our breakfast." Outside the room she washed her face in the basin by the wall. She slipped into her clothes and combed her hair. In a minute her bed was rolled and put away upon the shelf. "I was dreaming such a funny dream just now when you were shaking me," she said. The room will do, she thought. I can sweep it later. Sera Sensei may not come to look at it today. Then down the narrow stairs to breakfast they went. The other girls were at the table. One of the big girls read the Bible and prayed the morning prayer. Masako had never come to understand what these girls were saying or what it was they meant. She had been to the temple with her father in her country village many times. But there was never anything that sounded in the least like this. Here they always sang a hymn together at the breakfast table. She liked the tunes, but the words meant nothing to her. Of course she bowed her head when all the others did and said "Amen" when the others said it. But she did not understand what god this was they prayed to. She wondered why there seemed to be but one. This morning when she thought of this she almost laughed out loud, thinking of all those little gods she had left dancing on her mother's kitchen floor before waking.

She wondered as she bent above her sewing why the things she thought about always led her home again. Perhaps it was because there were so many people there to think about. Her mother and her father, grandfather and grandmother; her oldest brother and his wife and their two children; two younger brothers and a sister besides Baby Sister, all these at home in that one house! No wonder the gods thought it a good place to live. Besides, she had two older brothers in the army. She was proud of them. She had a letter all her own from one of them just yesterday.

Shizuko San's father was in the army, too. He was an officer. He had been away from home since Shizuko San was six years old. Her mother must be very lonely with just Shizuko San's little brother to keep her company. Just four of them when they were all at home. Why, that was just the same as no family at all. Poor Shizuko San!

My, but breakfast was a long time ago! Sewing made her hungry. Or maybe there had been too little breakfast. It never was a long meal at its best, and now the morning prayer took longer than the eating. All through the prayer this morning she had been hoping that her class could stay at home today, and here they were. She had hoped to stay because she did not want to miss singing. Now with all the trouble she was having with sewing she almost wished they were out somewhere sweeping, digging, anything but sewing. Maybe if she took her sewing home with her tonight Shizuko San would help her with it. Shizuko San could really sew. The things she made always looked so neat, and the teacher always praised her. It must be almost time for this hour to be over. Here came the teacher now to check the work she had done. A whole class hour, and she had not even finished this one seam! She spent too much time thinking about other things. Her thoughts were always leading her to trouble. The next time she had sewing she would not think at all. She would just sew. "Masako San," Sensei was saying, "You hold your needle wrong. Here let me show you." With a heavy sigh and a little shrug of resignation Masako concentrated on the needle.

Over in the college building it was chapel time. The bell for class dismissal had just rung. Along the three floors of the building, doors were opened. Through them girls poured out into the halls, down the wide stairs into the chapel. Shafts of sunlight from the windows on the east fell upon the polished floor and lit up the backs of the brown wooden benches on the aisle nearest the open windows. A part of each long cushion showed a faded mustard green where the strong rays of sunlight fell. The girls marched down the aisle, into the benches row after row until all of them were filled. Harue was the last to find a seat this morning. She had been in the class on Chinese Classics, always the last class to be dismissed. The Sensei did not seem to know what a dismissal bell was for. No matter where he was when the bell rang he always went a little farther. When they were finally free to go, Harue could not find her hymn book. When she found it she hurried into the last place on the last bench in the room.

It was so very warm this morning. How glad Harue was to sit for this half hour. She liked the new way of having all the service sitting down, especially on these summer mornings. It was so dark back here that she could close her eyes and nobody would notice. She had not slept enough last night. She had to catch the five o'clock train or she was late to school. That meant that she was up each morning by four-thirty. She tried to get to bed by nine o'clock each night, but sometimes lessons made this difficult. Last night she had studied until after nine, and then she had written to her brother. He was fighting somewhere in the South Pacific. They had never known just where. She knew he counted on her letters. They had always been such friends. She mailed the letter on her way to school this morning. In the last letter that had come from him he seemed so very upset about them all. He had been thinking about harvest time and how his father needed him. He was the only son and their father was not well. The farm was all they had to live from. Her brother was the one who wanted her to go to college. He had found out about the examination they gave for scholarships. She had taken it and won a scholarship. This was her second year. Her brother wanted her to finish college. He was very proud of her. The letter last night had been hard to write for she had to reassure him. He had enough to think about without the extra worry about home. She hoped she had succeeded. She had written:

To my much esteemed elder brother: Now that August is here and the weather has become so very warm, I trust that you are taking every care to keep yourself in the best of health. You may put your honorable mind at rest about those of us here at home. Father, Mother and I are all quite well, as usual.

I do not know what time it is with you, but here it is now ten o'clock at night. Father and Mother are already fast asleep. My bed is spread upon the floor, and I am sitting here beside it at the desk where you have so often spent the evenings studying and where I have been working on my lessons for tomorrow. All the lights are out except the shaded study lamp here on the table. In the dim light I can see outlines of the bushes in the garden, the stone bench under the old pine tree, and the dark mass that is the bamboo grove beyond. The clover is in bloom, and it is beautiful this year. From the big bush at the corner of the house comes the sound of the night insects we have listened to together on so many summer evenings. There is no other sound save the rustle of my paper as I write.

The village has changed greatly since you left. There are no boys here any longer. Just last week the last five went into training. Hayashi San and Kubo San went to the navy. The others are in the regular army. We had a big village send-off for them. It reminded me of the one we had when you and the other boys were leaving.

On the first day of each month Father, Mother and I make the rounds of all the shrines to pray for your safe-keeping. We are proud to have someone so brave as you fighting for us in this war. We pray always that the gods will keep you safe; that you will perform with honor your duty to your nation and your Emperor; and most of all that you will be able to return to us before too long. Every day our mother goes to pray at the new Soldier's Shrine. Every evening just before the dark comes I go, too.

Harvest time is here again. Father misses you very much, but please set your mind at rest. I am only a foolish girl and cannot fill your place completely, but you can rest assured that I am doing everything I can. I have already been at work in the fields beside our father, and I shall help him every day until the crops are in. I am home from school each day by three o'clock.

I go into the fields at once. Today we have been gathering the soy beans. The crop is not too good because it has been dry all summer. There are two rows left to gather. I shall finish them tomorrow afternoon. Do not think I am forgetting about my promise that I made to stay in college. I do my studying at night when it is too dark to work outside and when I am on the train those two hours every day.

So please put your heart at rest. I have made up my mind to take your place and mine while you are gone. All will be well with us. Please keep yourself from being wounded. Father and Mother both send their love. And now for this time, Sayonara.

Your Little Sister

Harue wondered whether she had said enough to ease his mind. There was so little that anyone could say. One could not write that all of them were hungry all the time now; that the rice crop looked poorer than it had in years; that every day the air-raids came a little closer and filled their souls with fear. The teacher on the platform had begun the morning prayer. Harue bowed her head. She too would offer up a prayer to this foreign Christian god. In Bible class the teacher said this was the god of all men everywhere. "God, keep my brother safe and bring him home to us again," she prayed. And now the last hymn was announced. "Hikari ni ayume, yo" -- "Walk in the light" -- Strange to sing of light when everything around seemed full of darkness. Perhaps this was the meaning of the word "Faith" that she had heard so often in school. Seeing light when there was no light to see. Acting as if there were light when there was only darkness. She must take her Bible home with her and read it some time out of class. "The Lord bless thee and keep thee. The Lord cause His face to shine upon thee and give thee peace" the choir was singing. Harue rose to lead the line out of the chapel.

CHAPTER 10
EIGHT-FIFTEEN

As chapel in the college began, Mori San and Hata San were nearing Hijiyama. They had not walked fast because the heat was too intense. They had taken the streets that led along the right bank of the river because there was more shade there in the mornings. Each had been intent upon her own thoughts. Hata San was thinking about Gaines Sensei. Dead 13 years. It seemed impossible. She still saw her every day in some familiar place, on campus paths, along the school halls, in the garden at Gaines Hall, or most often in the big wicker chair inside the living room. How quiet that living room had been the day Gaines Sensei died! Not Hata San. She had paced the kitchen floor for hours -- after the doctors said there was no hope, and while the girls and teachers from the school marched single file up the front stairs, through the hall past Gaines Sensei's door to make their last low bow to her. Once Hata San had gone into the living room. It was full of teachers who had taught long for Gaines Sensei. One was sitting by the fireplace in Gaines Sensei's chair. Sera Sensei scarcely touched the chair at all, so straight she sat, eyes lowered, hands folded in her lap. Yamada Sensei stood beside the Chinese table, gazing out the window at the drab February day. Even here the padding of those never ending steps in the hall above had followed her. Back again into the kitchen. There were fewer people there. Suddenly the padding sound had ceased. Upstairs a door closed. Then Mori San's slow step upon the stairs, the opened kitchen door. "Gaines Sensei is dead," Mori San said.

Somehow they had not thought about Gaines Sensei's dying. She was as much a part of things as the buildings on campus or the house she lived in, something that would last as long as the school that she had built. Those three short days of illness had not been long enough to change their set of mind. The loss of her had staggered them. One thing had been clear to all of them. Gaines Sensei must be buried in Hiroshima. Now the memories came in quick confusion. The violets she had picked from underneath the snow to place in Gaines Sensei's white hand. "He leadeth me, oh blessed thought," sung in English at the service at the house. The farewell from the graduates that Yamaguchi San had read at the big funeral. The closing of the oven door at the crematory. The sheen upon the earthen jar that held the ashes. The cleanness of the plain white box. The lot on Hijiyama with the pine trees growing round it. The smoothness of the plain gray stone.... This morning they must look to see if that last azalea they had planted was still growing. There was almost too much shade on that side of the hill.

Mori San thought of Miss Rachel. She was thankful that she had not failed her. She had given her the thing she wanted most in all the world, that she and "Sister Nannie" should rest side by side upon this quiet hillside. This sounded simple when you said it, but it had been the hardest thing she had ever had to do. Those two years, 1941-42, had been her trial years. Not even the hardships of this war as she had seen them in Hiroshima had taken from her soul the anguish and terror she had known before. There had been weeks of indecision in the spring. Miss Rachel kept saying, "Shall I go or shall I stay?"

"You must go," her foreign friends said.

"Stay if you wish," Mori San and all the others at the school said. "We will see that no harm comes to you."

And then the final word, "I cannot go unless Mori San can go. She has no passport." Those frantic weeks of waiting for a passport. The suspense. Would there really be a war? Then many things in quick succession. The arrival of the passport. The packing, things in boxes to be left here in Hiroshima, things in boxes for the U.S.A. Miss Rachel all the time protesting, "I had rather stay right here to die. If I go now I shall never rest on Hijiyama."

But they had gone, in the spring of '41. The hardest thing for Mori San had been to leave her friends here at the school. There had been that last morning at the train. Then Kobe and the big boat and anxious days on the Pacific. Then California. For awhile, there were days of calm and beauty when the threat of war seemed far away from them.

Then suddenly it was December 7. War. She had not thought that it would come, but now she was an alien in enemy territory. Fear struck her soul. But there must be no fear that anyone could see, especially Miss Rachel. And so Mori San went about her days those first weeks of the war with her mind set only on the things that came to hand. There must be no thought about the future or about the present outside this small house and this garden where she lived.

Friends had made their Christmas very gay that year. Fears were pushed aside. Miss Rachel had seemed very happy, but Mori San could feel the anguish in her mind. Then one January morning the quick pain in Miss Rachel's head, sudden unconsciousness, and before night time she was gone. The memory of that awful emptiness made her so weak even now that she stopped a moment in the middle of the street. Hata San was busy with her own thoughts and did not see.

Mori San insisted that the body be cremated and the urn stored. The ashes must be taken back to Hijiyama. When or how she could not see. She only knew that sometime she or someone else would take them there. She was questioned many times by the officials, but they were never unkind. They let her stay with friends for those first weeks. These friends then put her on the Grispholm. She was sent back to Japan with other enemy aliens, and her heart was sad. She was happy, though, in one thing, and that made her willing to face hardship if it came. With her she carried the precious urn that held Miss Rachel's ashes. It would rest on Hijiyama by Gaines Sensei's side.

Then Mori San was back in Kobe after the longest year she had ever seen. To get the ashes into Japan had not been easy. Plain clothes men followed her all the way back to Hiroshima. The Secret Police had taken over there. There were hours and hours of questioning. And after that, "The Shadow." He was probably somewhere there behind her on the road this morning. But now she did not care. A host of "shadows" could not shake her satisfaction in that she had kept faith with her friends.... Why, here they were already at the bridge. The walk this morning had not seemed half so long as she expected it to be.

"Hata San," Mori San exclaimed, "look where we are."

"Yes," said Hata San. "We have surely kept our thoughts in our own heads this morning. I like to cross this bridge because from here we can look all the way out to sea. How blue it looks this morning. Even from here, Miyuki Bridge looks much bigger than the one we are on. I suppose they will build a new one here some day. This must be the oldest one in town."

"The bridges seem so full this morning," answered Mori San. "From here we can see three, and all of them are full of traffic. I suppose at this hour of the morning most traffic always moves toward the center of the city. We have so little to keep us company, moving out the other way."

Across the bridge they turned into the narrow path that led up to the cemetery. At the caretaker's house they stopped just long enough to get a bucket and a trowel. Then they climbed slowly up the winding path that led them to the top of the green hill. At the cemetery's edge they paused and turned to look down on the city they had left.

The city, a living, breathing thing. At eight o'clock in the morning alive in every throbbing street, in every narrow path and alleyway. Alive under every gray-tiled roof and along each gleaming waterway. Alive with men and women whose bodies moved along the streets, in and out of buildings made of stone, concrete or wood. Men and women whose hands and feet were agile, hesitant or slow at tasks imposed or self-appointed. Men and women whose minds moved in designing, hour on hour, this day that was beginning; in building up yet other days, tomorrow and tomorrow. A city of soldiers. Thousands of them. Trains spewed them out at the railway station and left tired drooping masses of them standing with their packs and rifles on the ground beside them. Soldiers, marching six abreast, shoulders sagging, steps uneven, on the road between the railway station and the city port five miles away. Soldiers, driving trucks of ammunition or supplies from factories to big ships that waited for them. Soldiers, new recruits, drilling for the first time on the West Parade Ground. Soldiers, shooting big guns at targets on the mountain-side across the East Parade Ground; practicing with bayonets beside Misasa Bridge, --- wild shouts, running figures, bayonets thrust deep into the straw men ranged along the high bank of the river. Soldiers, looking arrogant and pompous behind piled desks in wooden buildings in the castle grounds. Soldiers, hurrying in and out the castle gates, fat brief cases and fluttering papers in their hands. Soldiers, standing guard at factory gates, in stations, in front of barracks, and at each entrance to the castle grounds. Soldiers, working in the barracks mess-halls; grooming horses in the stables; washing ragged undershirts, dirt-gray underpants and long white gee-strings in the shallow river water beneath the Soldiers' Bridge. Soldiers, lying maimed and broken in long low hospital wards, swathed in bandages, arms and legs swung in slings above their beds, eyes desperate, arrogant, dull with pain, no eyes at all. A city full of soldiers by the thousands. But there were others, too. There were merchants, men and women in a hundred different kinds of shops and hundreds of each kind, scattered through a sea of gray-tiled roofs. Factory workers, men and women, two thousand here, three thousand there, who ran the huge machines in war plants and manned munitions factories. There were office workers, women for the most part after these eight years of war. They sold the tickets in the railway stations; sold stamps and postal cards, weighed parcels, postmarked letters in the city's post-offices; served as tellers in the city's hundred banks; sent, received and delivered telegrams; worked as secretaries, clerks, office "boys" in business firms, in courts, in Prefectural and city halls. There were scores of doctors, interns, nurses who manned the scores of municipal and private hospitals; ear, nose and throat hospitals, eye hospitals, bone hospitals, hospitals for internal diseases, for infectious diseases, for women's diseases, hospitals for tuberculosis and for syphilis. There were doctors trained in Germany, in Tokyo and in Kyushu. There were doctors of the old school who gave hot baths and massage, who used the red hot needle as a cure for every ill, who meted out queer herbs and powdered snakes as medicines. There were midwives who furnished rooms in their own homes for lying-in. There were restaurant owners and the keepers of hotels with their corps of waitresses and maids. People worked in houses rich in precious woods and unique carvings set in lavish landscaped gardens; in houses built on modest streets where rooms were cheap and dark, but clean; in boat-houses on the rivers, two-storied, gay at night when lights from the papered doors made golden splashes on the black moving waters; in cheap juke-joints along narrow, noisy streets filled with the stench of rancid frying oil, decaying fish, bad liquor and cheap scent. On this day as on every day at this time in the morning policemen walked their beats; coolies, men and women, pulled their carts or led their horses through a hundred different streets, hurried here and there on errands, or, standing in long lines, unloaded barges at a river's edge; housewives went about their morning shopping with their babies on their backs while they pushed the baby buggies full of purchases; some went about their morning tasks within their straw and paper houses; mothers nursed lean hungry children from lean yellow sagging breasts; old women fondled crying children on doorsteps in the streets; laughing children played around them.... To Mori San and Hata San on the hillside looking down upon the city it seemed quiet, almost asleep, save for the distant humming that rose to them through the blue-gray mist of heat.

"This afternoon," thought Hata San, "I must be at the hospital by three."

"Tonight I must remember to water the lilac tree," thought Mori San, "and tomorrow I must see about the piano that Yamada Sensei spoke about."

Together they turned to walk between the stone markers in the cemetery, and in a moment more they were seated on the stone bench that faced Gaines Sensei's grave. Mori San looked at her watch to see how long the climb had taken. "Just eight-fifteen," she said aloud to Hata San.

Eight-fifteen at Gaines Hall. Yuki San had brewed herself another cup of tea. She took the tray and went outside to rest on the bench beside the fig tree. Her morning work was done, and she was just a little tired. How full the fig tree was! There were a few figs ripe on the branches where the sun could reach them. As soon as she had her tea, she would like them for her lunch. Too bad there was no sugar. She would like to make some fig preserves....

The French clock chimed eight-fifteen, and Kihara San wrote on. It seemed so hard to stop this morning. She would have to send this letter in two envelopes. Two letters would make Sa-chan very happy. How calm and cool the garden looked! How lonely it would be without the cicadas! She must not make this letter any longer. That pile of sheets was waiting to be mended. She could finish them before time to go to the hospital this afternoon....

Eight-fifteen on Hondori. "This is a noisy street," thought Tamako San. "I must hurry home where it is cooler and more quiet. I can help Kihara San mend the sheets and the mosquito nets.... That looks like the china that I want, that piece there on the back counter in this shop." She stepped inside and took the china bowl up in her hands. "The pattern is the same but the blue seems different...."

Eight-fifteen in the Willow Gardens. The perspiring manager sits behind his desk working at his piles of papers. In a small room in the rear his wife knelt on the floor. A square of matting stands beside the wall where she placed it. She takes up a loose plank from the floor on which she knelt and lifts from the hole a large metal box. Unlocking it, she raised the lid and placed the sack her husband gave her with the others it contained....

Hana Chan lay exhausted, half awake and half asleep. "It is too hot to sleep these August mornings," she complained aloud. She thought, "That old fool, Kihara. What a beast he is. I thought that I would never get him in this morning. I have never seen him half so drunk." She raised her hand to let a ray of sunlight strike the diamond on her finger. The old woman servant slipped noiselessly into the room. She said, "Your friend Kihara has a head this morning. I have put him back to sleep." "Look," said Hana Chan, holding out her hand. "Last night he gave it to me. Will you put it in the bank today where you have put my other things? Here is five yen. You may keep it all." The old woman laughed and tucked the money and the ring inside her obi. "Some day," she said, "you will get caught...."

Eight-fifteen in Asano Park. On the mound at the east end of the garden Ojii San stooped to dig the weeds from the gravel path. Then he raised himself to rest his back and looked across the garden and beyond where the castle gleamed between the tall pine trees. What a perfect picture it would make! If only he could paint it! This afternoon he must take the castle road again on his way home. The moat should be full of lotus blooms by then. He bent again above the gravel path....

Eight-fifteen at the bath-house by the bridge in Haku-shima. Ojii San's wife, Obaa San, was at her morning bath. She squatted on the drain boards with her little wooden tub beside her. She rubbed her wrinkled skin with vigor. Her shriveled breasts swung pendulous before her. Seated on a low stool beside her, her friend, the green grocer's wife, lathered herself with a bold extravagance. "How good your soap smells," Obaa San said. "Just look at mine." "Use some of this," her friend replied. "I will bring you a whole new cake when we come for our bath this evening. My husband knows where to find all kinds of things. He never puts them on the shelves, of course, just sells them -- for a price --to certain customers. I will bring a cake to you if you will tell no one where you got it." Obaa San nodded toward a younger woman on the other side of the big sunken tub. "Look at that hussy there. Another baby on the way, and her husband these three years away, fighting somewhere in the army. How long since those last soldiers were billeted with us here in this neighborhood? She had three of them with her...." "Yes and it would probably be hard to tell which one the child belongs to," replied her friend. "Or, I hear that Mr. Baba from that paper store just up the street goes in and out of her front door at all hours of the night." "It will go hard with her if ever her own man comes home. She is far too pretty to be good...." and the two forgot their bathing as their heads came close together, and their voices buzzed like the droning of the cicadas outside.

Eight-fifteen in Ojii San's house. Ayako San had finished breakfast, returned her rice bowl and her chopsticks to their accustomed place upon the kitchen shelf, and prepared herself for sleep. It was far too hot to put the pallet on the floor. The matting would be cool. She hoped Tajiro would not work too long in this hot sun. He was not strong these days with so little food to eat. She folded her work clothes and wrapped the white cloth that served as her sole undergarment tight about her waist and hips. She lay down, delighting in the roughness and the coolness of the matting against her skin. She closed her eyes and thought, "If I could only sleep..."

Eight-fifteen on the West Parade Ground. The work Tajiro San had done had been inspected. The boys stood in two long lines before the shrine and bowed together. Then they stooped to lift their brooms and rakes up to their shoulders and turned to march in double file along the hot, unshaded streets. No word was to be spoken until they reached the school. Tajiro felt again to see that he had not lost Dannie's money. He took it from his pocket....

The general in his office inside the castle walls rubbed his smooth head in perplexity. He could not understand the orders that had poured into his desk this morning. Before an order could be executed, cancellation orders came. All these orders that he issued and then changed must make him seem a complete fool. He was thinking, "I have known for some time that this war was being bungled. If I could only get to Tokyo...."

Eight-fifteen and the old woman was at home again. Home in summer was the boat house tied with strong ropes to the piles beneath Sakai Bridge. Her husband rented rowboats for the river. His little fleet bobbed up and down at one end of the boat houses. The business had held up as well as any in these times. While the old woman peddled groceries for the green grocer just across the bridge, the old man carried on here at the boat house. Just now the old woman returned. Her feet were tired from walking on the burning pavements. She was sitting on the edge of the low deck, her feet dangling in the cool river water. Her husband checked the rowboats across the deck from her. "August is the worst month of the year," she said. "This morning I could feel the heat right through my wooden clogs. It is good to get back to the coolness of this water...."

Eight-fifteen in the little village, Ushita. In his house beyond the village Yamada Sensei told his wife about his morning as she helped him change from his wet crumpled uniform to a black and white checked house kimono. "Mori San looks thin," he said. "I sat with her in the garden for awhile this morning. I told her she and Hata San should walk out here tonight when it is cooler. Perhaps if they come soon enough we can all walk up the mountain. There is always such a good breeze at the top...."

At the Petroffs in the village Dannie's work was finished until Tajiro came. He was playing now with neighbor children in the street outside the garden wall. Sandra and her mother heard their shouts from the veranda where they sat. The two of them were shelling beans they had gathered last night from the garden. The beans were hard and dry, but they would make a meal. "I wonder," Sandra said, "if we will know our Niki when we see him next. He must be very tall and handsome, I should think." "He was always very handsome," Mariya answered her. She heard her husband saying, "I shall see you then next week." The lesson must be over. "I must go in and get my ironing done," she thought. Sandra spoke again, "Mother, do you suppose...."

Eight-fifteen at the school. Sera Sensei turned from the bookshelves in the corner to meet the cook who stood waiting for her. If she could only shake off this foreboding that oppressed her! She thought, "I wonder what there is that we can eat today. Perhaps if I could go out to the big market...."

Masako folded up her sewing and put her needles in her sewing kit. She hoped that Shizuko San would not mind helping her tonight. "And now I am all ready for the singing class," she thought....

Harue stepped out of the chapel door into the hall. She was humming softly to herself, "Walk in the light...."

9. Worship service in school chapel - 1931.

CHAPTER 11
A NEW REALITY

Now Ojii San was standing at the river's edge saving frantic children and crazed women from sure death in the river. He soothed them with his words and guided them with steady hands to open spaces where they could lie down. Now and then sharp pains shot through him. He did not know just what had happened, but he knew that this was war. He was his own commander; he knew the ground he fought on; he gave his orders and saw that they were carried out.

Kihara San died with the white folds of her letter to her son still lying on the floor beside her. One instant of intense, surprising agony, and that was all. For her husband, still asleep in the Willow Gardens, there was only nothingness.

The manager lay pinned beneath the heavy beams that fell upon him. He heard the crackling of flames as they came nearer. He could see the smoke that rose in swirling eddies up above him. He heard the cries of women all around him, "Tasukete kure, tasukete kure!" Once he heard his wife call out in a long anguished cry, and that was all. He watched the flames come toward him with a kind of weird detachment until the heat was so intense that he knew nothing more.

Hana Chan pulled herself free from the debris over her. There was a numbness in her face. Needles of pain shot through her when she put her right foot on the ground. Dazed, she joined the line of maimed and stumbling human wreckage that moved to no place, only out of the place they were. Hondori had its moving line of wreckage.

Tamako San was not a part of it. She lay in what had been a china shop. From the piles of porcelain dust and splintered wood one white hand protruded, a piece of broken china in its palm. No one would ever know the names of those charred, naked bodies in the bath house.

Ayako San, blood streaming from her face across her bare full breasts, became a part of the sluggish human stream that flowed across the bridge beyond the burning ruins of her house toward the green hills in the distance. Her son, Tajiro, lay upon another road far away, his charred fingers wrapped tightly round the little bit of money that belonged to Dannie. Near him on the West Parade Ground lay piles of what had been the new recruits for the Imperial Armies. Others that would never fight now, some blinded, others burned or lame, moved about in crazed bewilderment. Only the stones of the castle walls remained as they had been. The general no longer thumbed the papers on his desk in nervous irritation. He was a part of the smoke and flame that rose within those walls of stone. The castle keep-tower was no longer there to look down on the bustle of the city. Its white walls had become a part of the white cloud that hung in heavy frothing billows high above the ruined city.

The old woman at the boat-house, for one bewildered moment, raised her hands to shield her eyes from the sudden flash of light. The boat-house rocked as if an ocean wave had struck it. Not knowing how she got there, the old woman found herself swimming in the river. Swimming was not easy with her mompei fastened tightly at her ankles. She saw that she was near the rocky ledge beneath the bridge. She turned in that direction. "How strange things look," she thought. "That great cloud hides the sun." She pulled herself up on the rocks, exhausted from her efforts in the water. She saw her husband swimming toward her. She helped him to the rocks beside her. She looked around her and saw the river full of people. "Look at all the people in the water," she exclaimed.

"They are dead people," said her husband.

She looked again and saw that he was right. Then she looked beyond the river and saw the flames and smoke. "What awful thing has happened to us?" she asked her husband.

"I do not know," he answered. "All I know is that these people here are dead. We are alive. There must be work for us to do."

"It is the gods I prayed to earlier this morning that have saved us," the old woman said with awe. "Come, let us go up to the bridge. The gods will show us what to do -- we who are the living among so many dead." Together with slow, careful steps they made their way up the steep path onto the bridge.

Across the river, Mr. Petroff stood beside his gate. In Ushita there had been that sudden flash of light, some tiles had fallen from the shaken houses, here and there a wall lay crumbled, but for the most part, the destruction was no more than a small earthquake would have brought. Mr. Petroff watched the long line coming from the city with horror growing in his eyes. Now and then he touched someone he knew upon the arm and led him through the gate to Mariya and Sandra who stood ready with as many bandages as they could find. They dressed the wounds as best they could and sent some on their way again. Others stayed to lie in dazed agony on the cool matting of the floors inside the house. In the wicker chair on the veranda, Dannie lay unharmed, but frightened and bewildered. When he had raised himself from the ground after the bright light had passed, he saw two of the children he had been playing with. One was lying crushed beneath a stone pillar that had fallen. The other's head was lying open where the sharp edge of a falling tile had struck him. Dannie had been sick beside the roadway, and then rushed home to Mariya's waiting arms. Mariya had comforted him a moment and then left him to lie quiet where he could not see the horror of the passing line. Mr. Petroff recognized Ayako as she passed him. She staggered as he reached her. He picked her up and carried her to the veranda where he laid her gently down. "We will keep her here," he said, "until we find Tajiro."

Yamada Sensei stood looking at the mushroom cloud that hid the sun. "I must go at once to see about the school," he told his wife who stood beside him. "Get the house in readiness; our friends may need us." He hurried down the road. He stopped a moment at the corner to look down at the stone Jizo San that lay prone upon the ground, his face buried in the dust beside the road, his many bibs awry. He stopped again a little farther down the road to talk with groups of villagers that stood stunned beside the road. And then he saw the surging stream that poured out from the city. He wondered how to get into the city. It seemed one solid flame. He hurried on to meet the stream before him.

On Hijiyama, Mori San and Hata San dropped to the ground, heads buried in their arms to shield their eyes from the quick flash of light. They braced themselves against the stone bench when the wind came. When it had passed they rose, shaken, but still whole. With trembling, hurried steps they made their way back to the point that overlooked the city. Where there had been a sea of gray tiled roofs spread out beneath them there was now only climbing flame and boiling smoke as far as they could see. The past fell from them. There was only now this wild burning present. Above them hung the surging cloud, black, yellow, rose and snowy white. The white brought memory again to Mori San. Aloud she said, "Hata San, the white lilac tree!" Hata San replied, "The roots will live." There was no way to go down into that burning city. "I think," said Hata San, "if we could get across the top of Hijiyama we could take the road down on the other side. Then we could work our way around the edges of the city all the way to Ushita. By the time we get there the fires will have died down, perhaps, and Yamada Sensei will come with us to the city. We must not stop to think now. Let us go." Bewildered and afraid they turned to make their way to the other side of Hijiyama.

The city was no longer sure of anything. It felt its heart pulled out and up into that rising cloud above it. Into the cloud passed the spirit of the city she had been. The past had melted and dissolved into the nothingness of smoke. The present was a horror, pointing with thin flaming fingers toward a nothingness that was tomorrow. Tomorrow? Could there be tomorrow? "As long as men and women walk my streets with aspiration in their souls I shall not die." This had been her thought this very morning. Could aspiration live through hopelessness and ruin? Would men's souls stir again? There were so many things that could not live again. The castle with its shining dolphins, broad eaves and white walls would be no more. It could not live again because for long years it had been a shell with no life in it. Could the thing that it stood for live and grow to bring destruction on itself again? Always when war had destroyed, war had grown up again.... The ancient temples could not be again as they had been. They were a part of yesterday that had dissolved to nothingness. Was there a living root within them that would grow and flower again?.... Her stores, homes, schools, hospitals, parks, trees, flowers - all ruins. Thousands of her men and women dead or dying.... But thousands lived.... If hope lived on in them beneath the desolation, there could be tomorrow. But no tomorrow could bring back the part of her that was already dead. She had been the city of the living; in one swift moment she had become the city of the dead. No matter what her hope was for tomorrow, she would always be remembered as the city that had died. Through all her broken streets she groaned in anguish. She could not know that through her travail a new era had been born. The Atomic Age had come.

10. Ruins of Girls' Middle School - 1945.

11. Ruins of Specialty School of Higher Education - 1945.

CHAPTER 12
FORWARD WITH HOPE

In the late afternoon of an October day Yamada Sensei climbed to the knoll on top of Ushita Mountain. He sat down on a stone to rest. The day had brought him greater satisfaction than he had known for months, or was it years? Time had ceased to have a meaning since that August morning when the world had changed. He did not often let himself think back. The horror of that day and night and of the days and nights that followed was still too real to contemplate. Someday, perhaps that horror too would fade. There was at least a satisfaction in having done what they had done today. He rose and walked across the knoll to a new wood marker. This morning in a brief but solemn ceremony they had put it there. It marked the place where they had buried the ashes of the more than 300 girls and teachers who died in the smoking ruins of the school that August morning. On one side of the marker was the date and the number who died. On the other side was written, "I am the Resurrection and the Life..." Yamada Sensei felt one thing accomplished. The dead were honored. They could turn now to the care of those who lived. He stood another moment with head bowed; then turned into the winding mountain path and disappeared into the deepening shadows.

As he hurried toward the lights that sprang up in the valley below him he was thinking of another satisfaction that the day had brought. Today the school had opened in an unused building here in Ushita. He had taught again today, and it was good. More students came than there was room for. There were no books nor charts nor maps to teach with. Teachers were not many. Some of the best would never teach again. They were the ones who rested there upon the mountain top. But school had started. In spite of all the "nothingness" the school would grow again.

He could see the lights of his own house just below him. He remembered telling Mori San how glad he was that he had moved to Ushita. That was in the garden at Gaines Hall the morning the bomb had fallen. Now it made him very happy to have a house full of the teachers from the school. All of them had nothing, as the school had nothing. Two of them had died in his house of the "peculiar sickness" that took its toll in the weeks that followed that first holocaust. Mori San and Hata San were living in his house and would stay until the school had found a way to build new dormitories. Then Hata San would take the place that Sera Sensei left in the high school dormitory, and Mori San would be the matron for the college girls. He had still been in the city on that night when Mori San and Hata San finally made their way to Ushita from Hijiyama. His wife said they were dazed with the agony that they had seen along the way. It was in the early morning hours of the next day that he reached his home again with the three or four teachers from the school who seemed wounded worse than the others. Two of them they carried on crude stretchers made of boards. Gradually a school community had built itself around him. People came and built themselves crude huts of any kind of salvage that would make a covering. They filled the rambling camp with dormitory girls and others who could not find their relatives. Many of them still were sleeping on the rough boards of the floor because there was no bedding for them. Some would never find their parents. Others stayed because their parents had no place to keep them and could not feed them. Food. That was the hardest problem now for all of them. The old woman who had kept the boats at Sakai Bridge came every morning now. She and the old man were living with a son somewhere back behind the mountain. She came down the narrow valley at the same time every day with her basket of green vegetables slung on her back. Sometimes she brought the only food they had. Her husband came now and then with fresh fish from the sea or from the river. He said one day, "Now that the war is over I think that I shall take up fishing regularly. There should be a living in the fish business. The sea remains the same in spite of this destruction."

"And we will buy your fish," Yamada Sensei promised.

He was home now, and it was time. The sun left this valley early, and the autumn chill came down with a quick suddenness. The evening meal was ready. Those who remained a part of the communal household were already eating, seated around two tables pushed together to make one. Yamada Sensei thought, "This house is like the houses of the early Christians where they had everything in common. It is a blessing in such times as this. One may feed his soul on fellowship and forget that there is little food to satisfy his body."

Mori San was saying, "Hata San and I walked up to Sera Sensei's grave today. It was a blessing that the temple there against the hillside was not burned. Sera Sensei would have wanted to be buried by her mother and father. It is so shady and cool there by the graves. Sera Sensei lies almost beneath the eaves of the old tea-house in the garden."

Yamada Sensei's wife said, "Did you hear about the woman who committed suicide last night? They found her on the railway tracks this morning just beyond Misasa Bridge. They told me at the rice store that she had been a geisha in one of the big houses that burned. Hana, I believe they called her. Her face, they said, was very deeply scarred and she had lost her hair. Poor thing! I suppose that she had nothing left to live for."

"A letter came this morning from the Petroffs," Yamada Sensei said. "They are well and very happy." His thoughts went back to the story Mr. Petroff told him on that day in late September. He said that in the afternoon he had walked into the city. There was no reason for his going except that Flowing River Street seemed to draw him. He had thought that he would go again to see the ruins of the house that he had lived in before he moved to Ushita. The street was a dead street in a dead city. All around him he could see no one except two U.S. soldiers walking toward him. He reached the ruins that had been his home. He turned to look at them once more. His soul was full of thankfulness that he had moved before that day. Behind him he heard footsteps. The two soldiers would be passing him, no doubt. Then the exclamation, "Dad!" He turned to see what voice had spoken. The tall G.I. stood still, his arms outstretched. "Dad, you do not know me. It is Niki, Dad!"... Niki had been searching for his family. He did not know that they had moved. He had come here where his home had been and there were only ruins. His heart was very sad. Today he had come once more before he had to leave the city. Perhaps he could find someone...and there he found his father in the middle of the street. "The kind of thing one reads about in fairy tales," Yamada Sensei thought. Now all the Petroffs were in Tokyo with Niki. Sandra and her father were working with the Occupation Forces, so this morning's letter said. "We shall miss the Petroffs," Yamada Sensei said aloud.

"Yes," said Hata San "we shall miss them all." She was thinking of her Mi-chan whose charred body they had found beneath the ruins of her house. The two babies were beside her.

Mori San was looking at the box that held the ashes of Kihara San. They were here to wait the coming of the son who had not seen the letter that she wrote that morning.

"Ayako San, may I have some hot tea?" Yamada Sensei called. Ayako San had been with them since the day the Petroffs left for Tokyo. They had never found Tajiro. Ojii San too had died. Yamada Sensei found him in the park that day, doing everything he could to make the wounded and the frightened comfortable. He somehow seemed to feel that all the people who had found the park a place of refuge in this time of need were his own personal guests. As their host it was his duty to see to it that they had his personal attention and his care. Although wounded, he had worked without a moment's rest far into the night. Sometime close to midnight, he and Yamada Sensei had bent together over one poor charred creature who kept calling for a drink of water. Suddenly Ojii San straightened with a long drawn sigh. When Yamada Sensei turned to look, Ojii San lay there at his feet quite dead. Now as Ayako poured his tea Yamada Sensei thought, "He was a good soldier. He fought a good fight, and he kept the faith."

Mori San was speaking, "I keep feeling that this defeat was necessary; that nothing but defeat could save us. Sometimes when I am walking through the waste that is Hiroshima I feel more than a little guilty."

"You need not feel that way," Yamada Sensei told her. "I have known for a long time that only through defeat could come salvation. Only a true democracy can save Japan. There must be no more bureaucracy, no more military power. We must be through with war. This defeat can bring these things to pass. Without it, they could not have come."

Mori San replied, "Today when we came back from Sera Sensei's grave we stopped to look again at the white lilac tree. We pushed aside a few more of the tiles that covered up the roots. The branches are all seared, the leaves are gone, but life is creeping up again into the stalks close to the earth. The roots are still alive."

"I told you that the roots would live," said Hata San.

"And now as soon as we can move it, we shall bring it here," said Mori San. "I would like to have it planted by the wooden monument we set up on the hill today. I think Gaines Sensei and Miss Rachel would like to have it there. The lilac tree that Mr. Petroff has given back to me I want to plant on the plot of ground where we will build the new Gaines Hall."

"The lilac did not die," said Yamada Sensei slowly, "because its roots went deep into the earth. That is why the school we love lives on. Its roots are deep within the hearts of all of us. The city cannot die because its roots are buried in the soul of men and women who will give it a new birth. We shall live to see the lilac blossom into white again. We shall see the school I dreamed of fill this mountain and the city with its good. We shall see a new Hiroshima, a city freed from military domination, a city in which freedom and democracy can grow. If this hope were not within me I should throw myself down from the mountain. God has given us a chance. May He give the wisdom and the understanding that we need to take that chance."

Hata San and Mori San wiped tears from their eyes, but through the tears a new light shone.

The city stirred again. She was still torn and anguished, but today she felt new life begin to stir within her. She could look up again, and out, toward a tomorrow. What another day would bring she did not know. She only knew that life still moved within her. Life would foster growth; growth that was small in the beginning but mighty in the end. What she had said upon that August morning she could say again with confidence and in that confidence was peace. "As long as men and women walk my ways with aspiration in their souls, I shall not die."

EPILOGUE

EVENTS DURING WORLD WAR II

E vents during the war and the results of the bomb on students, parents, teachers and the school are described in another book, *Summer Cloud, A-bomb Experience of A Girls' School in Hiroshima*. The book includes testimonies of three students, three parents whose daughters were killed, and three teachers. The book also includes commemorative messages by Hamako Hirose, President Emeritus, Hiroshima Jogakuin, and by Akira Ishida, President, Japan A-bombed Teachers Association; a thumbnail history of the fifteen year war leading to and including World War II; a description of the ordeals of those connected to the school during the war due to their ties to the United States; and steps of the peace movement. This book was edited by the English Department of Hiroshima Jogakuin High School and published by Sanyusha Shuppan. It is highly recommended and can be obtained from Peace Resource Center, Wilmington College (Ohio).

Mori San in Miss Johnson's story accompanied Miss Rachel to the U.S. in the spring of 1941. She was present on the January day when Miss Rachel suddenly fell ill and died. A short time later, Mori San returned to Japan with other enemy aliens and brought Miss Rachel's ashes back to Japan. Mori San arranged for the burial of Miss Rachel's ashes by her sister on Hijiyama. *Summer Cloud* describes the same event and tells that Miss Kobori was the person who came to the U.S. with Miss

Rachel Gaines, stayed with her in Pasadena, and brought her ashes back for burial on Hijiyama Hill with her sister.

One of the teacher's testimonies in *Summer Cloud* is by Kiyono Kobori who was living at Gaines Hall on the campus at the time the bomb fell. Unlike the book's character Mori San, she was not at Miss Gaines' grave when the bomb fell. Mrs. Obara and Mrs. Matsushita came to visit her about 7:30 that morning. Mrs. Matsushita was the wife of the Dean of the college. Miss Kobori was protected by the piano when the building collapsed. She helped her friends from the completely collapsed building, however Mrs. Matsushita did not survive her injuries.

All the buildings - the kindergarten, the high school, the college, the dormitories and Gaines Hall - at Kaminagarekawa-machi were completely destroyed and burned by the atomic bomb. The bomb, which fell about one-half mile from the school, killed 351 students and 20 members of the faculty. President Matsumoto and Dean Matsushita narrowly escaped from under the fallen school buildings, but each lost his wife. In *Summer Cloud*, President Matsumoto indicated that about 500 senior high and college girls were working in a factory outside of the city limits, freshman students of the College were having worship service, and more than 300 of the Junior High girls were gathered on the school grounds in preparation for the day's work when the bomb fell.

He tells how he found his wife and daughter walking from their collapsed house and left them at a nearby park while he returned to the school. There he rescued eight girls from the ruins of the college chapel, but many others perished in a fire which broke out in the ruins. The fire not only claimed the college building, but the lives of more than 100 students who could not be removed. He then went to the spot in the center of the city where the Junior High girls were working and found many of them annihilated by the blast, and others wandering around blinded by the flash of the explosion.

That evening, President Matsumoto returned to the park where he had left his wife and daughter, only to find his wife had died by the river when pushed down the embankment by a panicked crowd. In his testimony he said, "But she looked calm, serene and peaceful. Strangely enough, she reminded me at that moment of Orphelia in Shakespeare's drama Hamlet; so sad and so fair she looked. It is needless to tell you what an unbearable blow her tragic death was to me. She was such a devout, prayerful, peace-loving woman. Perhaps she died, together with many others, glad to be instrumental in bringing the war to a speedy end. At the same time, I feel that war, by killing such truly peace-loving Christians, has condemned itself as nothing short of utterly senseless folly."

He also wrote, "All the buildings of our own school were completely destroyed. Nothing remained. So many friends of the school, even some of the school leaders, said that this was the end of the school. But I felt otherwise. A school which had been started in the name of God and dedicated to the cause of Christian education should not be allowed to die out. I was determined to demonstrate that even the atomic bomb could not, should not, obliterate a Christian school like ours."

12. The Matsumoto family--Shigemi Matsumoto (son), Dr. Takuo Matsumoto, Mrs. Tokiko Matsumoto, and Yuko Matsumoto (daughter).

POSTWAR HISTORY
OF HIROSHIMA JOGAKUIN

C lasses were re-opened at the hillside site of Ushita in October, only two months after the tragedy of the atomic bomb, by President Matsumoto, Dean Matsushita and a handful of teachers. Less than 100 college and high school girls attended and school could only be held every other day because of poor health conditions and scant transportation. These classes were held in borrowed class rooms at a partially destroyed municipal elementary school in Ushita. The following spring (1946), barrack buildings were built as classrooms for college and high school.

The next year the Junior High School started under the new school system of post-war occupied Japan on the old site of Nagarekawa-machi. These buildings were among the first school buildings rebuilt in what was called "the Atomic desert of Hiroshima."

In 1948 a classroom building was erected for the senior high school at the Nagarekawa-machi site. At the college site, a library and a home economics building were constructed. A new classroom building was erected in 1950. In just five years, the school was once again offering its full program of education!

Dr. Hamako Hirose, a graduate of Hiroshima Girls' School, became the first Japanese woman president of Hiroshima Jogakuin College in 1951. At the same time, Miss Katharine Johnson returned to the school for 15 months as vice president while on a leave of absence from Wesleyan College in Macon, Georgia.

Under the direction of Dr. Hirose, the school continued to grow. The temporary barracks at Ushita were replaced in 1952, a junior high school classroom building was erected with administrative offices for the entire school in 1953, an addition to the college library and a home management unit for the home economics building were completed in 1954, followed by a gymnasium in 1955. The enrollment in 1955 was 198 in junior college, 232 in senior college, 657 in junior high school, and 703 in senior high school - a total of 1,790 students.

In 1962, kindergarten classes were added to the school for the first time since the war with the opening of the new Gaines Kindergarten facility in Ushita. In January 1964, a new senior high school building was completed.

Hamako Hirose--The story of Dr. Hirose is interesting. She was born in an outlying county of Hiroshima Prefecture on February 15, 1905. About 1920, the brother of Miss Nannie B. Gaines sent Miss Gaines $50.00 per year to be used as she chose. Through her official friends, she offered two scholarships on the basis of a competitive examination. The scholarship was offered in two counties in the Hiroshima Prefecture which had previously supplied no students. Eighteen girls took the examination and the highest one in each county entered the Hiroshima Girls' School on scholarship. Both were good students and went out as Christian workers. Hamako Hirose was one of these students. Her record was so outstanding that she was sent to America for further education. She obtained a B.A. degree from Central College, Fayette, Missouri in 1929. She then studied in Nashville, Tennessee at Scarritt College for Christian Workers, and obtained a M.A. in 1930 from George Peabody College for Teachers.

When Miss Hirose returned to Japan in 1930, Miss Gaines recommended her as a teacher of religious education to Lambuth Training School for Christian Workers at Osaka. She was made president in 1938 after serving eight years as Professor of English and Director of Religious Education. The school became Seiwa Women's Junior College in Nishinomiya in 1941 and she continued as president until 1951. Miss Hirose kept that school open during the war even though the missionaries were recalled and communications were cut off from the U.S. Students were trained and sent out wherever Christian work could be maintained during the war. After the war, she was one of the first Japanese selected by the co-operative committee in Japan and endorsed by the co-operating mission board, to come to America for building up her physical strength and for further education for leading her people in the Christian Way. Miss Hirose spent a fall term at Scarritt. She then attended Columbia University and was awarded the degree of Doctor of Education in 1950.

Although Dr. Hirose was an obvious choice for president of Hiroshima Jogakuin, she was reluctant to accept the position and asked for the appointment of Miss Johnson as a requirement for her acceptance. This was arranged, with the happy outcome that Dr. Hirose served the school as President of the college until 1974, and then as Chairman of the Board of Trustees until her retirement in March 1987.

Dr. Hirose was active in various organizations, including: the Board of Trustees of Seiwa Women's Junior College, the Councilors of the International Christian University of Tokyo, the Religious Education Committee of the Japan Church of Christ, the Board of Directors of the Japan Christian School union, the YWCA National Council and President of Soroptimist International of Hiroshima.

She received the honor of Distinguished Alumnae (1952) and the honorary degree of LL.D. (1966) from Central College. She also was honored with the Royal Medal of Blue Ribbon, Emperor of Japan (1968) and the Royal Medal of 3rd Order of Golden Crown, Emperor of Japan (1975).

Dr. Hirose died on April 23, 1988 at the age of 83.

13. Girls' Middle School Students beside the Temporary Auditorium at Ushita - 1947.

14. Dr. Hamako Hirose President Hiroshima Jogakuin 1951-1974.

HIROSHIMA JOGAKUIN TODAY

Enrollment at Hiroshima Jogakuin in 1993 totaled 3,150 - 1,500 in the colleges, 750 in Senior High School, 700 in Junior High School and 200 in Kindergarten. The faculty numbers about 200 and the Alumnae Association has 25,000 members. The Junior and Senior High Schools remain in the center of the city and the Kindergarten, Junior College and College are about two miles north of downtown on the edge of the city in the hills.

The following description of the present day school has been abstracted from the school brochure, *Hiroshima Jogakuin, 1987*:

Hiroshima Jogakuin Gaines Kindergarten - The kindergarten's goals are to develop good personality and habits, and to encourage individuality and independence. It has one nursery class and three classes each of 4-year-olds and 5-year-olds, for a total of about 200 children. The kindergarten started accepting handicapped children in about 1977. These children have been integrated into classes with good results for both groups.

Hiroshima Jogakuin Junior and Senior High Schools - The school grounds include a carefully tended 30-year-old arbor of cherry trees which gives a traditional Japanese welcome to students. The number of families with three generations who have attended the school is increasing. Most students live at home, however about 60 students live in the dormitory.

School starts with a worship service accompanied by the pipe organ. Bible classes are held once a week. There also is a week of activities devoted to special religious and philosophical concerns, where international brotherhood and peace based on Christian principles are emphasized.

Each of the Junior and Senior High Schools have a three-year program. In Junior High School, the goal is to cultivate habits of studying independently and mastering basic learning techniques. Senior High School classes help students prepare for further study. Throughout the three years, students are trained in written and spoken English by native English-speaking instructors. About half of the students, upon recommendation of the High School, continue their education at Hiroshima Jogakuin College.

The Junior and Senior High Schools have their own student governments. Every year a festival is held on Culture Day and an athletic meet on Sports Day. Various other committee activities are sponsored all year round. Club activities include publishing a newspaper, interscholastic sports competitions, music recitals, drama presentations, etc. The students learn how to serve others through volunteer work with the handicapped, visiting rest homes, etc.

Hiroshima Jogakuin College - The Junior College consists of a Culture and Living Course, Home Economics Course, and a Nutritional Science Course. The fundamental knowledge of Domestic Science and Culture is taught with emphasis placed on their applications. It aims at developing independent and practical women with a broad outlook. In the Home Economics Course, a License as a teacher of Home Economics in Junior High School or as a Secretary may be acquired. In the Nutritional Science Course, a Dietician License may be obtained, and in the Culture and Living Course, a Secretarial License.

The Senior College (School of Specialized Higher Education) has an English Literature Department, with English and Japanese Departments. The aim is to develop in each student a good background in Liberal Arts as well as sufficient knowledge and ability in the major fields. Classes are kept small and seminars are also offered. Professors and students work together closely on research activities, particularly in the Japanese Literature Department. In the English and American Literature Department, importance is placed on the teaching of practical English, including debate, by native-speaking specialists. In both Departments, there is an Education Division where a Teaching License for Junior and Senior High Schools can be earned.

College students lead an active campus life by participating in club and circle activities. Particular attention is paid to the field of music where the choir, as well as folk song, mandolin, rock music, musicals and "koto" groups, sponsor a colorful variety of activities. The choir has been on a concert trip to the U.S.A. The sports clubs are also very active, and have succeeded in maintaining a high ranking in intercollegiate games. Many students take part seriously in volunteer work, which is a special characteristic of this College.

About 70% of students graduating from the Literature Department obtain immediate employment and almost all of the Junior College students find work upon graduation. Some become teachers or civil servants, but the majority work in banks or company offices, including mass communication areas. The number of graduates who pursue a lifetime career is increasing, although the majority become homemakers. In the home they have a keen social consciousness and many join in volunteer work. Some graduates pursue further study in graduate schools or go abroad to study.

Alumnae Association - The Alumnae Association strengthens fellowship among graduates, offers scholarships to students and helps the school raise memorial funds. It remains an association for Bible study and recreation among the teachers and graduates, continuing the tradition nurtured by Miss Nannie B. Gaines. Headquarters are in Gaines Memorial Hall on the Senior High School grounds. There are 30 chapters of the

Association including ones in Hawaii and Los Angeles. Reunions are a source of encouragement for alumnae living abroad.

15. Cherry trees in bloom on the High School grounds.

16. A Junior High School and Senior High School worship service.

17. Junior College and College campus at Ushita.

18. Gaines Hall Alumnae Building - 1953 Officers of the Alumnae Association, left to right Mrs. R. Kawamura, Miss K. Kobori, Mrs. T. Yamasaki.

PREWAR HISTORY OF
HIROSHIMA GIRLS' SCHOOL

T he school was founded by Rev. Teikichi Sunamoto with the collaboration of Methodist missionaries, Dr. and Mrs. James W. Lambuth and their son and his wife, Dr. and Mrs. Walter R. Lambuth. Soon, Miss Nannie B. Gaines joined the school from the United States, beginning a long and influential period with the school. The following background information will help the reader understand these persons and groups.

The Japanese Mission of the Methodist Episcopal Church, South - Although Christianity was originally introduced to Japan by Spanish and Portuguese missionaries in about 1550, it was forbidden in 1637 when the government ordered all foreign influence removed. Religious freedom was restored in 1873 during Emperor Mutsuhito's Meiji (Enlightened Rule) reign. In 1886, the Methodist Episcopal Church, South sent missionaries to Japan. Dr. and Mrs. James Lambuth, their son and his wife, Dr. and Mrs. Walter Lambuth, and Dr. O.A. Dukes came from their work in China. The mission they founded became known as the "Mission of the Inland Sea".

The Lambuth Family - James William (Dr. J.W.) Lambuth, the son and grandson of American Methodist ministers, was dedicated as a missionary at birth. He became a Methodist preacher, although he also studied law and medicine. He was married in October 1853 to Miss Mary Isabella McClellan of New York after preaching for one year in Mississippi. A few months later, he and his wife volunteered to go to China as missionaries. They arrived in Shanghai in 1854 and worked in China for 32 years before helping to found the mission in Japan in 1886. Dr. James Lambuth died in 1892 and his wife a few years later. He was buried in Kobe, Japan and she in China.

Their son, Walter Russell Lambuth, was born in China and was the fourth generation missionary in the family. He attended school in the U.S. and then returned to China as a medical missionary. He married Daisy Kelly, the daughter of a missionary. They came to Japan in 1886 following service in China. Dr. Walter Lambuth later returned to the U.S. as Missionary Secretary of the church. He was elected a Bishop of the Methodist Church in 1910 and was in charge of Methodist missionary work in China, Japan, South America, Africa, Europe and parts of America. He died in 1921 and was buried beside his mother in China.

Other members of this family were involved with mission work in China. Walter's sister, Nora, married Dr. W.H. Park, medical missionary in China. Their daughter, Margarita, married Dwight L. Sherertz. They started work in China in 1918.

Rev. Teikichi Sunamoto - Teikichi Sunamoto was born September 30, 1857, and grew up seeing boats and ships in the harbor and in the rivers of Hiroshima. His father died when he was young and he had no interest in traditional learning. The lure of the sea and far off places was strong and he left his family at the age of 17 to sail the seas. Some years later, he was walking the streets of San Francisco and met a Japanese Christian, Date San, who took him to the Gospel Society of the Salvation Army. Sunamoto San entered night school and for the first time came in close contact with Christian people. He studied the Bible eagerly, and through the influence of workers in the Chinese and Japanese Mission was converted to Christianity. He was baptized and spent three years learning English and telling others of Christianity. He burned his pilot's license to prevent his life on the sea from interfering with the call of Christianity. He is quoted as saying in a meeting in San Francisco, "I have no learning, I have no worldly wealth; but I have Christ in my heart, Christ in my head, Christ in my bones, and I must tell it."

Teikichi Sunamoto returned to Japan to tell his mother about Christianity. He arrived in 1886 with a letter of introduction from Bishop Harris of the Methodist Episcopal Church. The letter asked the Methodist Episcopal Mission in Yokohama to send a missionary to teach his mother. Unfortunately, Yokohama was more than 400 miles east of Hiroshima, and no one there was available to help at that time.

Mr. Sunamoto then heard of the Southern Methodist missionaries in Kobe and traveled there to ask their help. He saw Dr. James W. Lambuth and Dr. O.A. Dukes and they agreed to come as soon as it could be arranged. Mr. Sunamoto continued to his home in Hiroshima and busily spread the word about Christianity. After a few weeks, he sent reports of positive response to Kobe. Becoming impatient, he followed that with a more urgent letter and finally sent a telegram, "My mother is praying. Come."

Dr. James Lambuth and Dr. Dukes arrived in October of 1886, soon after receiving the telegram. Mr. Sunamoto joyfully told them of the results of his efforts. This included the interest of a school teacher who taught 160 boys and a Buddhist priest with 250 pupils.

Dr. Walter Lambuth and his wife, Daisy, soon were also helping Mr. Sunamoto start the school. They sent an urgent call for a missionary lady to come to Hiroshima and take charge of a girls' school in a church paper in the U.S. Miss Nannie B. Gaines saw the paper, offered to go and was accepted. Her coming to Hiroshima proved to be instrumental in fullfilling Rev. Sunamoto's dream.

Rev. Teikichi Sunamoto died on May 7, 1938, nearly 52 years after founding the school.

Nannie B. Gaines - Margaret M. Cook told the story of Miss Gaines in *Nannie B. Gaines, Missionary to Hiroshima and to*

Japan. Miss Gaines was born in Kentucky in 1860 to Gustavus C. Gaines and his wife, Elizabeth Cromwell. She was christened Ann Elizabeth. Her name was changed by family usage to Nannie Bett, and this later shortened to Nannie B. She was seven when her father died, just when she entered the village school taught by her mother. Nannie treasured her father's and grandfather's books in her search for knowledge. The family sacrificed so she could attend college in Franklin, Kentucky. She remained close to home after graduation and helped her family meet financial needs by helping on the farm and teaching school.

When her mother died, Nannie followed a younger brother to Florida. She was elected to a college position at Leesburg in 1886. After her first year, just before she left Leesburg for summer study in Chicago in 1887, she read the urgent call from Walter and Daisy Lambuth for a missionary lady to take charge of a girls' school in Hiroshima, Japan. She had heard about the Lambuth's ten years earlier when a college friend told her of attending the wedding of Daisy Kelly to Walter Lambuth. She told her that the young missionary doctor, born in China, was sailing back to China with his bride. Nannie's imagination was stirred by the story. She secretly responded to the request of the Lambuths, offering to go. Late in the summer, a letter which was delayed in delivery reached her in Kentucky. The letter was from the Board of Missions of the Methodist Church. It accepted her as a missionary and appointed her to the girls' school in Hiroshima. Three days later she was on a train for California. On the way, in Kansas City, Nannie sent telegrams to her family, and to the school and church friends in Florida. She was concerned about their feelings about her leaving with such short notice, but she wrote, "I dare not do otherwise lest my courage fail to break the home ties." She sailed September 1 from San Francisco on the steamer, City of New York, and arrived in Japan on September 23, 1887.

Soon after arriving she wrote, "It was the sympathy and love of the Lambuth family that helped me get a vision of what it meant to be an ambassador for Christ." She said after a mission meeting "I am sorry that every missionary cannot be a first recruit to a new, small mission. There is something inspiring in the fact that faith and trust in God are the only means to success."

History of Hiroshima Jogakuin before 1946 - As earlier described, the Lambuth's helped Mr. Teikichi Sunamoto open a school for women in Nishi-daiku-machi, Hiroshima City on October 1, 1886. In the following year, the school was called Hiroshima Eiwa Girls' School.

Miss Gaines arrived in 1887 and began class work the morning after her arrival, with 30 women waiting to be taught. She wrote, "The pupils (a group of about 30 mothers and daughters) were eager to see the new teacher. What a helpless, useless individual the new teacher was....What a cause for thankfulness that Mother Lambuth had made a plan and organized classes." Soon a school for girls was begun with seven students in small, dark, rented rooms in a Buddhist temple.

Miss Gaines became principal in 1889. Government recognition of the school was obtained in 1891. In October 1891, the new school buildings, built just the year before at Nagarekawa-machi, burned down. But a week later, Miss Gaines opened school again in a temporary building to the utter amazement of some of the citizens who believed that she would return to America as a failure.

In February 1893, the attached kindergarten was founded as the first of its kind in that part of the country. The school buildings were built on the Nagarekawa-machi site in September, and in the following year an elementary department was added to the school. The institution now included three flourishing departments - kindergarten, elementary and high school.

In 1897, the name of the school was changed to Hiroshima Girls' School and another kindergarten was opened in another part of the city. Kindergarten teacher training also started about this time.

A college department was added in 1919. Mr. S.A. Stewart was appointed principal, and Miss Gaines became principal (president) emeritus. The alumnae association was also organized in 1919 by the graduates.

In 1921, the Kindergarten Teacher Training Department was combined with the Bible Woman's School established by Mrs. J.W. Lambuth in Kobe. The combined school was moved to Osaka and became the Lambuth Training School for Christian Workers.

In 1928, Gaines Hall was donated to the school by the alumnae members. It was built as the dwelling place of Miss Nannie B. Gaines who was then living with her sister, Miss Rachel Gaines.

In 1929, the first Japanese president, Rev. Zensuke Hinohara, succeeded Mr. Stewart who retired for health reasons. Rev. Hinohara's election met Miss Gaines' goal to transfer control from the missionaries to the Japanese. Jubilee Hall was dedicated as the main building of the college department that year.

In 1931, the institution was renamed Hiroshima Jogakuin and the college department was officially recognized as a college by the government. On February 22, 1932, the school held an all-day celebration. Miss Shannon, a long time missionary at the school, wrote, "It was a great day. So many of the alumnae came. Miss Gaines was very happy." The day was cold, and Miss Gaines became seriously ill that night with pneumonia. She died the afternoon of February 26. Apparently aware of the war that threatened Japan and the world, her dying words were "We have touched the outside, but we haven't touched the inside yet!"

Miss Gaines had served 45 years at the school at the time of her death. My aunt, Katharine Johnson, was living in Gaines Hall at that time and told of Miss Gaines' ashes being located on the fireplace mantle following her death until approval could be obtained for her burial in Japan. In May, her ashes were buried on Hijiyama, a mountainside overlooking the sea and Hiroshima, home of the school and people she loved so dearly.

In December 1940, seven of the eight American missionary teachers returned to the U.S. They were Miss Shannon, Miss
Johnson, Miss Cooper, Miss Finch, Miss Anderson, Miss Spaul-
ding and Miss Tarr. The last teacher, Miss Rachel G. Gaines, left
Kobe on the last repatriation boat in April 1941, accompanied by
Miss Kobori. Miss Gaines was very reluctant to leave as she
wanted to stay in Hiroshima and be buried on Hijiyama mountain
with her older sister, Miss Nannie B. Gaines.

In 1941, the Pacific War broke out. During this time the
elementary department was obliged to close in 1942 and a group
of narrow minded citizens had public meetings accusing the
school unfairly. Rev. Hinohara retired in 1942 and was succeeded
by Mr. Takuo Matsumoto as President. The school managed to
continue with classes and chapel services. It gained the respect
and support from many of the thoughtful citizens.

19. Dr. James W. Lambuth

20. Mrs. James W. Lambuth

21. Dr. Walter R. Lambuth

22. Rev. Teikichi Sunamoto

23. Nannie B. Gaines when she started for Japan.

24. Hiroshima Girls' School Students - 1887.

25. First Kindergarten Building - 1891.

26. Primary Students - 1895.

27. Faculty and Pupils in front of Kindergarten Building - 1911.

28. First Kindergarten Teachers Training Class in Hiroshima.

29. Mothers of Kindergarten Students - 1917.

30. Alumnae of Hiroshima Girls' School - 1917.

31. Time for Play.

32. Later that day on the River Road.

33. Festival at the School.

34. The Hiroshima Jogakuin Family seated, left to right - Miss Nannie B. Gaines, Miss Katharine Shannon, Miss Ida Shannon standing, left to right - Miss Kobori, O Ai San (maid) Dr. Janet Miller, Miss Aunice Siler, Tanaka San (cook).

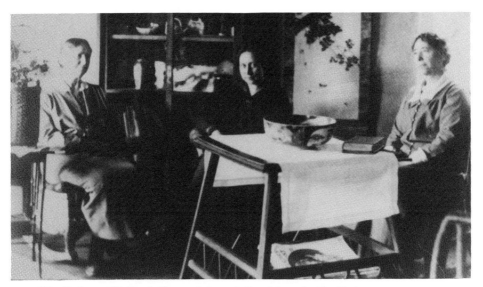

35. Gaines Hall - left to right - Miss Nannie B. Gaines,
Miss Katharine Johnson, Miss Rachel Gaines.

36. Eight missionary teachers in 1940 before return to the United
States Miss Johnson fifth from left, Miss Ida Shannon 2nd from
right and Miss Rachel Gaines on right.

ADDITIONAL INFORMATION
about
MISS NANNIE B. GAINES

An article by Harrison Collins, *A VETERAN REVIEWS THE WORK, An interview with Miss Gaines of the Hiroshima Girls' School*, published April 1930 in The Japan Christian Quarterly included this passage:

"It seemed natural to begin with the subject closest to hand and dearest to Miss Gaines' heart: the education of Japanese women. What were some of the desiderata for its improvement, I asked.

'Less official interference!' came the instant response. 'Despite the efforts of Professor Palmer and the rest, English, as conceived by the Department of Education, might as well be a dead language. Here's Miss Johnson just back from America and full of ideas that she can't carry out for lack of time due to official restrictions. There's too much translation of stilted texts and there's too little practical English. Why, mighty few Imperial University graduates could write an English letter our fifth-year girls wouldn't be ashamed of. You'd think the authorities would finally realize of themselves the handicap that this ignorance of fundamentals places Japan under on all occasions demanding the use of a foreign language. But they don't seem to care in the least, and go on teaching English as though it were a branch of logic or philosophy. I envy Mrs. Hani of Tokyo, who publicly states that her school tries to prepare its pupils for life and not for examinations.'

'Have you a similar complaint to make against the regulations governing the purely feminine side of Japanese education?'

'No, not at all. The standard of women's education in this country is constantly advancing. When I came here very few girls completed even the primary course; but now that manhood suffrage is a fact, with the franchise for women in the offing, it is only a matter of time before facilities for women will equal in every way those already provided for men. With that point gained, and the Confucian idea that to be a good wife and mother is the sole aim of woman abandoned, a general cultural levelling-up must come. Indeed, even now it is chiefly in the matter of English that we suffer; and if all the Mission-supported schools were to memorialize the Department and set forth their special qualifications for teaching real English, more freedom might possibly be granted.'"

Harrison Collins' interview resulted in this quotation when Miss Gaines was asked of her opinion of weak spots in Japan missions generally,

"The great waste in mission work lies in denominationalism, which may have had some excuse once but has precious little now. Also, there are altogether too many conferences over nothing. We ought first to get down to work so as to have some real experiences to talk about. Over-organization and a Soviet-like love of committee meetings are other drawbacks of the modern system."

When asked of the future of missions in Japan, she said:

"I am by no means a believer in quitting at this stage of the game. Missionaries will long be needed as advisors and as upholders of standards. Hitherto they have themselves been leaders, a role hard to give up.... We should limit our future direct evangelistic efforts to training leaders, and break new ground only in out-of-the-way places, or ways, where others cannot or will not venture."

Notes on Miss Gaines written by Margaret M. Cook indicate, "She lived through two wars, the war with China in 1894-

95, and the war with Russia in 1904-05; and her last days were filled with apprehension concerning the disturbed conditions of the hour. She believed in the Japanese and their potential leadership of the Orient, but she feared unless the leadership could be Christianized and she bemoaned every ascendancy of militarism.

Through the school her contacts were wide and she followed up her graduates even into Korea and Manchuria and China, seeking every opportunity to cultivate good will between the countries. In recent years she made two trips through Korea to Manchuria and Northern China, for the express purpose of strengthening ties between Christians of the three nationalities.

In a letter written in the summer of 1931 from Peking, China, from the home of an influential Chinese woman, her long-time friend, Dr. Kim, Miss Gaines told of their joy in bringing together Chinese and Japanese friends to talk and pray together. In writing to Dr. Goddard as late as November 1931, she says, 'There seems to me no hope for this part of the Orient except in the carrying out of the principles of Christ by our Christians. In my contacts with the three nationalities I have found perfect unity among the Christians of the three countries when they are brought together as brothers in Christ. Opportunities and experiences of the past few years have convinced me that this is the greatest work missionaries can do at this juncture; help the Christians to see that nationality cannot keep real followers of Christ apart.'"

When Miss Gaines was asked by Harrison Collins as to what she thought had occasioned her own remarkable and long-sustained success, she would only say:

"When you have a job just stay by it.... It is little by little that builds the house.... There's too much shifting around nowadays; Nobody seems to have any roots.... Some people have said that I had no nerves; but the truth is I had so many of them that I simply had to put them in a box, lock it up, and then sit on it."

37. Nannie B. Gaines

THE AUTHOR
AFTER WORLD WAR II

Miss Johnson switched from Dean of Women to English teacher at Wesleyan College in Macon, Georgia following World War II. She held the position of Professor when she left the school in 1954. She was granted a 15 month leave of absence from June 1951 until September 1952 to serve as vice president at Hiroshima Jogakuin.

In addition to her duties at Wesleyan College, she spoke extensively for the Methodist Church from Maine to Florida, east of the Mississippi River. Her engagements included mission study classes, Schools of Missions, talks for churches, women's organizations, etc.

She was a well liked member of the faculty of Wesleyan College during her time there. In 1946, this dedication was in the college yearbook:

"Because she is all the color and personality that is our theme, because she's warm and human, the one who knows there's something wrong without being told, the one who can give advice without being 'bossy,' we love her.

She came to Wesleyan a freshman with TRI-K, she's given us more than we can ever express in mere words and made a Wesleyan for us that no other dean could have.

Since memories are our sweetest possessions, we'll have in her one we'll always want to keep. In appreciation, Rivoli Campus dedicates its share of the VETERROPT to Miss Johnson."

In the library at Wesleyan, atlas stands were given in her memory in 1968.

188--Katharine Johnson

She was vice president of Hiroshima Jogakuin during a leave of absence from Wesleyan College in 1951-52. She sailed on the ship, Young America, from San Francisco June 11 or 12, 1951. On July 9, 1951, soon after arriving in Hiroshima, she wrote this letter to her friend, Miss Fannie White at Wesleyan College in Macon, Georgia, with instructions to "Pass this around to those interested:"

"Dear Friends All: I have been in Hiroshima about 10 days now and have thought of you often, but have been too busy to tell you so. There has been no adjustment time for this job. I have jumped right in. I got off the boat at 8 P.M. one night in Yokohama and was in Kobe by 10 A.M. the next morning for a conference with the out-going and in-coming presidents. Then I came on down here and was welcomed most royally. There are many old friends left in spite of all the years and all that has happened. They have really opened their hearts to take me in. They have made me feel much more one of them than I ever felt before. They say, 'You are going to be here for such a short time that we must enjoy the time as much as we can!' They have really visited me out. I have been out for two meals every day since I got here. My friend Kobori San, whom you have heard me talk about, is afraid I'm going to get really fat and she doesn't like that. I have promised her that as soon as I get into my own house I will eat sensibly. The trouble is that I will have to begin entertaining and that won't help any.

As soon as my baggage arrives I am going to move to the seaside. Dr. Hirose, the president, and I are going to live in the same house, but she won't be here until the middle of August. I am moving in right away. The house is Japanese, of course, but it is very convenient and comfortable looking. It has a beautiful garden and just beyond the garden is the Inland Sea with its islands and sailboats. It is quite a distance from the school but I can't imagine a more beautiful place to live. When I am settled I'll send some pictures.

The college closed Saturday for the summer. The Sr. High closes next Wednesday (July 18) and the Jr. High is out on the 20th. I imagine my vacation will be as busy as school time. There is so much to be done. I am overwhelmed every time I think about it. Can you imagine a school, with 1,700 students that has grown up from scratch in six years? It seems incredible. You can understand that there are lots of loose ends that have to be caught up. There are four buildings that must be started in the fall.

The city of Hiroshima is a city again. An enormous amount of building is going on. The streets are still terribly torn up, but they are all being widened and beautified. Friday afternoon I was taken to the Governor's office, the Mayor's office, to all the newspaper offices and to all the other colleges and the University here in the city. I really met the people of importance - the V.I.P.'s of Hiroshima. You should have seen me with my white gloves, etc., Japanese cards in hand. It was very interesting and I met some very nice people. Most of the people are very cordial. Now and again I sense a stiffened spine when I sit down by somebody on the street car or bus. My paper is giving out. I suppose Thommy and Boots [Dorothy Thom, her friend with whom she shared an apartment and their dog] are at home by this time. I wish I were, too. Much love to all.

Katharine"

In a letter November 23, 1951, Dr. Hamako Hirose wrote Miss Margaret Billingsley, Board of Missions, Methodist Church. She said, "First I must thank you for sending us Miss Johnson. Her coming to us has already meant so much for changing the whole atmosphere of the school into something warm and good. She has been a great help to me personally as I had to start on my new duty here. Teachers, students and graduates all are showing a good cooperative attitude to their new president, as poor as she is, and I am finding my new job a worthwhile one."

In a letter of August 9, 1952, Dr. Hirose said to Miss Billingsley, "First I want to thank you for the wonderful service rendered to our school through Miss Katharine Johnson. Her stay here during the 13 months meant to all of us a blessing. She helped to build many buildings, to improve college curriculum, to revise student association's rules, activities, and, etc. The Student Center was established through a gift of Wesleyan College students through her. She taught 12 hours weekly along with all the administrative work. She gave her full time and more to individual students who wanted to have her advice. Her long experience of life in Japan with the Japanese made it so efficient and successful, not mentioning her wonderful ability as a leader and good quality as a good teacher and well integrated Christian character with high scholarship. We were very proud of having her in our school. Students, teachers and everybody connected with the school want her to come back to Hiroshima again as a regular teacher, and we are certain that she will not disappoint us. Please see that everything will work out well so that she can make up her mind in spite of the hard pull she may feel from Wesleyan College."

Miss Johnson appears to have given serious thought to returning, but advised Dr. Hirose in June 1953 that she had decided to stay at Wesleyan one more year. When that year was concluded, she decided to take the position of Executive Secretary for the Interboard Committee (IBC) for Christian Work in Japan, located in New York City. The IBC was a group representing eight Protestant denominations[1] to funnel resources from those organizations to the United Church of Christ in Japan (Kyodan). The Kyodan combined about 60 % of Protestants in Japan and was formed following World War II. In 1957, the annual budget of the IBC approximated two million dollars and provided about 400 missionaries from the eight member churches.[2]

Miss Johnson's last trip to Hiroshima Jogakuin was in April 1958 as Executive Secretary of the IBC following a visit to Okinawa. She saw her friend, Dr. Hamako Hirose, president of the school at that time. She retired after five years with the IBC in January 1959 following exploratory surgery in December which showed untreatable cancer. She died at the home of her sister, Mildred Johnson Sims, in Jackson, Mississippi, May 21, 1959. She was buried in Fulton, Missouri, in a family plot with her father after a funeral service in Jackson. In addition to the services in the U.S., her friend of many years, Dr. Hamako Hirose, led the entire school in Hiroshima in a memorial service July 5th.

---

[1] Congregational Christian Churches, Churches of the Disciples of Christ, Evangelical and Reformed Church, Evangelical United Brethren Church, The Methodist Church, Presbyterian Church in the U.S.A., Reformed Church in America and United Church of Canada.

[2] The Interboard Committee (IBC) was replaced with the Japan-North American Commission on Cooperative Mission (JNAC) in 1973. The JNAC is located in New York City and coordinates two way mission activity between Japan and North America, and coordinates mission activities on common concerns between Japan and North America. Membership in 1994 in North America is: The Christian Church (Disciples of Christ) USA and Canada, The Presbyterian Church (USA and Canada), The Reformed Church in America, The United Church of Canada, the United Church of Christ, The United Methodist Church, and United Board for Christian Higher Education in Asia (associate member). Membership from Japan: The United Church of Christ in Japan (Kyodan), The Korean Christian Church in Japan (KCCJ).

38. Dr. Hamako Hirose and Miss Katharine Johnson.

REFERENCES

1. Cain, J.B., *From Pearl River To The Ends of The Earth, The Story of the Lambuths*, Mississippi Methodist Advocate. October 19, 1949.

2. Cook, Margaret M., *Nannie B. Gaines, Missionary to Hiroshima and to Japan*, Board of Missions and Church Extension, The Methodist Church 1949.

3. Cook, Margaret M., *Miss Nannie B. Gaines*, type written paper in files of Board of Global Missions, United Methodist Church.

4. Collins, Harrison, *A Veteran Reviews the Work, An interview with Miss Gaines of the Hiroshima Girls' School*, The Japan Christian Quarterly, April 1930.

5. Stevens, Julia Lake, *Knowing Interesting People in Hiroshima*, Young People, Board of Missions, Methodist Episcopal Church, South, April 1927.

6. Unknown author, several pages copied and located in scrapbook at Millsaps Archives, Jackson, Mississippi. These pages tell the story of Rev. T. Sunamoto and the beginnings of missionary work in Hiroshima.

7. *Summer Cloud, A-bomb Experience of A Girls' School in Hiroshima*, Edited by English Department, Hiroshima Jogakuin High School, Sanyusha Shuppan.

8. Imaishi, Masuyuki, Chairman of the Board, Hiroshima Jogakuin, Personal correspondence, 1993--1994.

9. *Hiroshima Jogakuin, Eighty Years of History in Pictures* commemorative booklet.

10. *Hiroshima Jogakuin, 1886 - 1986*, commemorative booklet.

11. *Hiroshima Jogakuin, 1987*, booklet about the school.

12. *New Patterns for Christian Work in Japan*, published by The Interboard Committee for Christian Work in Japan, probably 1957.

13. Hirose, Hamako, *Report, Hiroshima Jogakuin, Hiroshima, Japan*, April 1953.

14. Miscellaneous papers and correspondence, General Board of Global Ministries, The United Methodist Church, New York.

INDEX